THE FOLLOWING

THE FOLLOWING

JACQUELINE DRUGA

PRESS

Published by Vulpine Press in the United Kingdom in 2022

ISBN: 978-1-83919-439-9

www.vulpine-press.com

To my Godson, Steve. You inspired this book. How we all wish we could pull you through for one final moment.

ONE

THE LIGHT

"That's your third eye," my Baba would say.

I was all of ten years old when she first said that to me.

"You have a third eye, my little girl. A third eye."

With no idea of what that meant, I was certain she was making fun of a disability that I didn't know I had.

Was it a mole? A scar? Where was this third eye that I couldn't see.

Baba also had a way of doing, what my mother called, 'gin talking'. Maybe she only saw that third eye when she was three gin and tonics in. The same as when she saw a blue magic marker on the news anchor's face during the evening news.

"Wipe it off," she'd say. "They have people that do that."

Baba was old world. She came over from Europe when she was a teenager, and while I understood her English, everyone else had a hard time.

Except when she mentioned the third eye.

I never remembered her talking about my supposed birth defect until I was ten. Maybe she thought I was old enough to handle the abuse.

I broke down and told my mother that Baba was making fun of me, which was a hard decision for me to make. Telling my mother something bad about my father's mother just made her smile; just another reason for my mother to hate her.

But she explained the third eye thing to me. It wasn't the gin talking, it was my grandmother's 'crazy' beliefs. A third eye to people like my Baba was someone's ability to see or know things others do not or before they happened.

"It's an evil thing to believe," my mother told me. "If you do, you'll be in purgatory for all eternity."

I wasn't up on that 'purgatory' stuff, but I was pretty sure purgatory was temporary.

She explained to me that my great grandmother was a gypsy fortune teller who actually inspired Stephen King's novel *Thinner*, they just left out that it was based on a true story.

I wasn't sure how much of that was true. My mother and Baba had a constant battle. Both had their own versions of good versus evil.

I loved them both.

As I got older their fights were amusing.

After my mother explained the third eye thing to me, I told Baba about it and how I thought she was making fun of something on my face.

She laughed so hard and said, "No child, you have the third eye. The ability."

She explained all those times I remembered conversations that hadn't happened yet, or news stories that had yet to occur, the voices telling me things …

One time distinctively stood out to me.

It was family dinner at Baba's.

"It's a shame that spaceship blew up. Those poor people," I said. "So sad for their kids."

"Harper," my mother scolded. "Why would you say such a thing?"

Two days later it happened.

All part of that third eye.

It started making sense.

No wonder she kept asking me to find out a good winning horse at the track.

She wrote down in a blue journal all the things I said and when I said them, then next to them the dates it actually occurred.

"Have I been doing this all my life?" I asked. "I don't remember."

"No," Baba told me. "Ever since you stepped in the light. When you came back, you had the gift. And it will only get stronger."

Stepped into the light.

She was right. I did, and I was told I should never had made it back.

TWO

NEAR DEATH

I was nine when it happened.

With only a half block walk to the bus stop, my mother allowed me to walk alone. She stood on the porch though, every morning, even if it snowed. Coffee in hand she would wait there and watch me until I got on that bus.

That particular morning, it was chilly and foggy, typical early fall. I didn't want to wear a skirt. My knees were cold, but it was picture day and my mother wanted me to look my best in the class photo. She woke me up early to make my hair perfect. Pulled back on top and curled.

With my little windbreaker on, and a backpack far too big and heavy, I walked to the bus stop.

I was the only one that caught the bus at that stop. Like always, I kept looking back at my mother. She was there watching if anything would happen.

I wanted to wave once more, and I turned.

They say, the big bulky backpack saved my life.

That was the last thing I remembered, and then everything went black.

My mother often told the story how she watched in horror, and I never saw it coming.

Standing on that corner, my back to the road.

Mr. Jenkins wasn't paying attention. He had spilt his coffee and was too focused on that when he made the turn, cutting it too close and hitting me in the process.

I flew from her sight, she said, and then she took off for me. Screaming for someone to call for help.

I was dead.

Dead for several minutes and it was the bus driver who brought me back.

I don't remember that.

I do remember going from looking at my mother to black. Complete and utter black. That was only a second and I was moving.

Fast and furiously, shooting through a black void that suddenly lit up with streaks of light all around me. The lights moved as I did, like I was in warp speed in a Star Trek episode.

The intensity of their glow grew until I faced this brilliant and powerful light. It was so warm. I wasn't confused, I wasn't scared, I felt as if I was supposed to be there.

Blurry shadows of figures were in the light waving at me. There were no angels or pearly gates.

From the shadowy figures stepped my Uncle Earl. My mother's brother.

Uncle Earl had died a year earlier. At that time, when it happened, I didn't know how he died. Just that it was tragic, and he was young.

"Twenty-two," my mother would say. "He's gone at twenty-two."

But we never really talked about him much.

Uncle Earl always looked like a movie star to me. Perfect hair and teeth.

He waved and stepped to me. "Wait for it, Harper."

"Wait for what?" My voice was weird, echoing.

Even his sounded as if it came from underwater.

"You can't step any closer," he said. "Just wait for it. And Harper, tell them I'm here. I'm here. I didn't do it. If I did, I wouldn't be here."

"Huh?"

Crack.

Gasp.

I opened my eyes and was looking at my mother. She was crying and screamed out that I was alive.

I don't know what that noise was that snapped me out of it or back from wherever I was. It was hard to breathe, I was gasping, trying to catch my breath.

Every part of my body hurt. There was so much pain. I wanted to cry but it hurt.

Thankfully, I floated back to sleep, waking up in the hospital several days later with everyone around me. My mother, father, Baba and Aunt Connie.

The only recollection I had was waving to my mother and having that weird dream experience.

After I came to my senses and had some water, I told her about what happened.

"I saw Uncle Earl in my dream," I told her. "He said to tell you he was there, and he didn't do it; if he did it, he wouldn't be there."

My mother gasped, her face turned completely white, and she ran from the room.

"I'll be back, pumpkin," my father said, chasing my mother.

"What did I say?" I asked.

Aunt Connie stepped to me. "You—you saw Earl? In your dream?"

"I guess. I was waving to Mommy and after it was black, I was with Uncle Earl."

Aunt Connie stepped back, hand to her mouth and started to cry.

Baba moved to my bed and held my hand. "You rest."

"Baba, did I say something wrong?"

"No child." Baba shook her head with a gentle smile. "You said something everybody needed to hear."

THREE

UNCLE EARL

How it started is how it ends.

I don't know when I heard that for the first time, but it held true in my case.

My entire fourth grade year was spent in hospitals and rehab. I had to learn to walk again. I broke my leg and my hip. Both of which my mother claimed was the reason I wasn't tall.

I tried to catch up on schoolwork, but it was useless.

The near-death experience I had was the only strange thing that happened for a year.

Then the 'third eye' stuff began.

It wasn't all the time; I had no way to control it.

Once I realized what it was, I was forbidden by my mother to practice with Baba.

Baba surprisingly adhered to those wishes, telling me. "I am here to talk to and answer questions."

She kept writing things down when I would spew them out.

I could tell she wanted to tame me, fine tune these abilities she believed I got when I died.

Then around my thirteenth birthday, things made a switch.

I stopped hearing voices, sputtering out events yet to come and started having the strangest dreams.

When they happened, they were vivid dreams that made sense and in them, I was fully aware I was dreaming.

People would come up and talk to me. I didn't know them.

I was able to control when I woke up. If someone scared me, I snapped awake.

The scary people didn't come often.

They were nothing compared to when it happened when I wasn't in bed for the night.

If I was tired and tried to focus, or focused too much on something, it sent me into a hypnotic state and the dream would start.

Once in eighth grade math I was trying to focus on the teacher. Her monotone voice absorbed into my mind and suddenly, it was just an echoing voice in the distance, and I was alone in the classroom.

A man appeared. He looked like he was from some old movie. Hair slicked back, leather jacket.

He tapped me on my shoulder.

"Hey, do you have a second?" he asked.

I screamed.

I screamed so loud, I snapped awake.

The teacher was at the board, she looked at me and so did everyone in the class.

In the embarrassing silence, I claimed I saw a mouse.

I told Baba about it. I didn't know who these people were talking to me or why? It was driving me insane. I was grateful it wasn't happening every night, but when it happened when I wasn't in bed, that scared me.

"No longer focus for too long," said Baba. "It's causing you to go into a meditative state and in that state, you are lucid dreaming."

"How do I do that when I am trying to pay attention in class."

"Stop focusing on one object or one person. If you are listening to her instruction and focusing on that. Shift your attention, from the teacher to the paper to someone in class. You can listen but your eyes and ears cannot focus for too long on the same thing."

Admittedly, I tried the opposite to see if she was right in what was causing it.

I sat in my living room one day and focused on the science guy doing a television show. Listening to his words, watching only him.

Sure enough, it happened, my living room was transformed into some room from decades earlier. The television wasn't there. It was replaced with a radio.

I sat on a thick green couch. An ashtray was on the wooden coffee table before me.

"Hello," the pleasant woman's voice said. "My, don't you look lovely?"

Slowly I looked over my shoulder.

A woman in an apron smiled at me. The entire left side of her face was burned.

Instead of screaming, being scared, I simply said, "Wake up. Wake up."

I did.

Science guy was back on the television, my living room was normal.

Baba was right and from that moment on, I stuck to her advice, never letting it happen.

Of course, Baba was the only one I spoke to about it. I didn't dare mention it to my mom.

Until I didn't have a choice.

It was the last time in my youth that it occurred. Actually, it was the last time anything 'third eye' or ability related occurred.

A normal night's sleep, I was tired and after reading a little, I fell asleep, book on my chest.

What the actual dream was, I don't recall, but it went from the dream state of ridiculous subconscious dumping to a room.

A room I had never been in and the second I was there, I realized I was dreaming.

Then Uncle Earl appeared.

"You have a light about you." He waved his finger and smiled. "You are very hard to get near."

"I don't know what you mean."

"Your light shines for all to see and we all know."

"Know what?"

He shook his head. "Doesn't matter. I finally got to you. I need to get a message to your mom and Connie. My sisters need to know."

"Know what?" I asked. "I can't talk about you. I'm not allowed. They cry."

Uncle Earl lowered his head. "That's because they think I did it."

"Did what?"

"Harper, they think I killed that little girl. They think I did terrible things to her. I didn't. I just found her when I was

11

walking. I didn't know her. I didn't do it, I swear," he said sincerely. "Those men who killed me thought I did those terrible things. I never got a chance to say I didn't."

"Men killed you?"

"You didn't know?"

I shook my head and started to cry.

"Harper, listen to me. You have to get them to believe it, okay?"

"They won't listen because they won't talk about you."

"Okay, then I'll talk to your mom."

"How?"

"Take my hand." He extended it to me.

I took his hand and he squeezed it tight.

"Everyone knows you can do this," he said. "That's why they all try to talk to you."

"I don't understand," I replied.

"One day you will. Now wake up, Harper," Uncle Earl spoke softly. "Harper, wake up."

With a heavy breath, I opened my eyes and sat up. It was like I was holding all the air in my lungs and finally released it.

The book on my chest fell to my lap and when I reached for it, I saw Uncle Earl standing at the floor of my bed. He wasn't a solid form. Almost a slightly glowing holograph projection, desaturated some to remove color from his form, but around his entire body was a halo of colorful lights.

I gasped and scooted back. "Wake up. Wake up. Wake up."

"Harper, you're awake. Go get your mother. I have only a few minutes before I have to go back into the light."

I didn't move.

"Harper, go."

I flung off my covers, jumped out of bed and raced to my door. Before I left, I looked back once more to see Uncle Earl and then I bolted out.

It was still early in the evening; my mother was probably downstairs watching some late-night talk show.

I raced from my room and a soon as I turned the corner for the stairs, I saw her walking up.

"What's wrong?" she asked.

"Uncle Earl is in my room."

"Harper, stop."

"Mom, no he's there." I hurried down a few stairs and grabbed her hand. "He's there. He wants to talk to you, and he doesn't have time." I pulled her. "Please."

"Harper, you were having a bad dream, that's—"

"Mom."

"Fine."

She was reluctant. I was reluctant. I had just dragged my mother to my room, was it all a hallucination?

When we walked in, would he be gone?

Sure enough, the moment my disbelieving mother walked into my room, she nearly crumbled. Her legs buckled and she grabbed my dresser for support.

"Tina," Uncle Earl said. "Tina, I didn't do it. I didn't do it. Please know that. It wasn't me." He extended his arm. "Please know that."

My mother dropped to her knees on my floor. She let out this deep, hurt-filled wail, throwing her head back as she did.

From the corner of my room, like a bright star, a light appeared.

"I have to go," Uncle Earl said. "Please know I didn't do it."

He stepped into that light, looking once over his shoulder at me.

"Thank you," he said.

And when he stepped into that light, he vanished, and the light seemed to be sucked out of the room.

My mother sobbed.

She sobbed right then and there like I had never heard her.

She stayed on the floor of my room for the longest time, crying, saying nothing.

I thought we formed some sort of paranormal bond at that moment.

Perhaps we did. I would never know what she thought or how she felt.

She refused to mention that incident ever for the rest of our lives.

That was also the last time, for the longest time, that I had a crazy dream experience or anything 'third eye' related.

Until that day and the flood gates opened.

FOUR

FUNERAL FOR A FRIEND OF A FRIEND

I was convinced that the gift given to me when I died at a young age was gone. In fact, I was sure of it.

My mother hated it and at first thought when I had died that some sort of demon possessed me, enabling me to bring my Uncle Earl through from the bowels of hell.

Her words not mine.

I had to have gone to hell because Uncle Earl committed an unspeakable act and was beaten to death over it.

She took me to several priests and bishops and when they realized I not only could be in a church I could touch holy water. I wasn't possessed, I was more than likely suffering from a form of psychosis.

After a few hospital stays in my teens, I was sent to a special school for girls at a convent in Virginia.

Complete silence after eight at night. Medication before bed.

The medication allowed me to pass into REM sleep without ever lucid dreaming. Another medication stopped me from doing that focus trance I locked into.

Sometimes, I was curious if I went off the medication would the gift come back. I thought about it a lot over the years, until finally I thought I had my answer.

I started a new job at new restaurant. An upscale Italian eatery that offered benefits.

There was a lapse in my health insurance because of the new job and the medications were out.

Other than putting on a few pounds, nothing happened. No sudden trances or lucid dreaming.

So, when my friend Keith asked me to meet him at Brenner Funeral Home for the viewing of his friend, Rick, I said yes.

It had been before the final Uncle Earl incident that I had been in a funeral home or cemetery. I successfully avoided ever going to either. I'd make up an excuse, it was the flu, pink eye or lice. Things people knew were highly contagious.

If there was a service in a church, I would go. It was probably more a mental thing believing I was protected in a church.

Before the gift was lost, if I went near a cemetery or funeral home, I felt things, heard things and was scared.

That was done.

Two months off medication and nothing.

"Sure," I told Keith. "I'll meet you there."

I didn't want to spend my day off at a funeral home, but it was Keith asking.

It made sense that Keith didn't want to go alone. He didn't want to face Rick's mother. Keith felt partly to blame because he was supposed to meet Rick the night Rick died.

I told him that was ridiculous.

Rick was an idiot. He still would have gotten drunk and for the sake of a viral video, did a balance beam stunt on the railing of that bridge Only difference was if Keith was there, Keith would have jumped in the river to save Rick and I would have lost my best friend of thirty years.

We had known each other since we were seven. Keith was the only friend that wrote me weekly letters when I was in the convent.

The only friend that came to see me at the hospital and even though he was Jewish, went to weekly confessions with me because my mother said I had to keep a clean soul.

I wasn't sure when Rick came into the picture. Maybe during Keith's rockstar phase, but definitely before Keith wanted to become a social influencer.

Neither one of them were having any success. To me, they were both too old to be social media influencers. The last I looked Rick had forty subscribers and Keith had sixteen. Four of which were me, his mother, my mother and Baba.

At ninety-four years old, Baba loved Keith's videos. She laughed and watched them over and over.

I didn't get it.

The visitation time started at one and Keith and I planned to meet at three.

I arrived three minutes late and the parking lot was packed. I didn't see Keith's little smart car, then again it wasn't unusual for his mother to drive him.

He was the only grown man, pushing forty that I knew had his mother drive him so he could do videos in the car.

There were so many cars, I didn't think Rick had that many friends. Thinking he had a big family, I parked.

To the right of the door, roped off, was a long line of people. Some cried, some held their phones taking selfies with the funeral home in the back.

They were at a distance from the entrance, so I made my way to the front door.

A man in a suit stood there, I assumed he was a greeter until he stopped me.

"Friend, family or fan?" he asked.

"Fan? Rick has fans?"

"Mr. Cramer was a social influence star."

"Since when. Last I looked he had forty subscribers."

"Look again."

I pulled out my phone, searched him and gasped. "How does someone get a million subscribers in a couple."

"Create a viral video."

"Oh my God," I said. "Did the bridge thing go viral?"

"Yep. So, I'm going to take it you're family or friend."

"I'm support. I'm meeting his friend Keith here."

The man looked at the clipboard. "Keith's last name?"

"Levy."

He stepped aside. "Please go in. I'll warn you though. Fan visitation starts at four."

Considering the fact that I didn't see Keith and the greeter didn't mention that he was there, I sent him a text while my phone was out.

After I hit send, I put the phone in my purse. I was about to embark on a test.

A funeral home without medication.

I felt nothing. Heard nothing. It was a relief.

Before going into the main room with the open casket, I stopped at the visitor sign in book. I added my name, then decided to look to see if maybe Keith had come in earlier.

I flipped through the pages.

I saw his mother's name, Gladys Levy. I didn't see Keith's.

Another man in a suit approached me and whispered. "If you're looking for Beyonce's signature it's on the third page."

"Beyonce was here?" I questioned and quickly flipped the page.

"Yes, she's a big fan. Very torn up. This was tragic.'

"Yeah," I muttered, thinking, *avoidably tragic*. "It was. Wow." I saw her signature. "She was here."

He nodded.

But Keith was not.

I thanked the man, took a prayer card and made my way to the main room.

Would I feel something? Hear something?

There were a lot of people, tons of flowers, no Keith.

A woman stood near the open coffin, and I walked to Rick.

My heart pounded in my chest. It was the first soulless dead person I had seen in a long time. I stood directly at the coffin looking down to Rick. He wore a long sleeve tee shirt instead of a suit. His hair was weird, and combed down, unlike the product induced crazy hair he wore. But otherwise, he looked good.

I had to know.

I touched his arm.

Nothing.

I didn't know if I should have felt elated or sad. Suddenly I found myself hands on Rick's body, feeling everywhere I could.

"Were you close?" the woman standing by the coffin asked.

"Um, yeah. I just don't believe this is him."

She nodded. "I feel that. I'm his mother. Debbie."

I heaved in a gasp. "Oh, I am so sorry for your loss."

My phone bleeped.

"Would you …" I held up a finger. "Excuse me." I reached into my purse and pulled out my phone.

A text reply from Keith. 'Not coming."

"Asshole."

"Excuse me?" Rick's mother asked.

"Not you, not Rick. Keith." I held up the phone. "He's not coming."

"Good. My son is dead because of him."

I didn't know how to respond to that. I lowered my hand down. "I'm sure Rick doesn't blame him." Just as my hand rested on Rick's arm, I heard a voice. It was a man's voice and not his mother's.

"You don't think?" the male voice said.

With a slight shriek, I lifted my hand.

"What's wrong?" Debbie asked.

"Nothing. I … I have to go." I put my phone away. "I need to kill Keith."

FIVE

JUST TRY

Keith was exactly where I expected him to be. In his basement family room, sitting center of the couch, controller in hand, staring intently at the video game he played.

When he wasn't in front of his computer or walking around wearing that headgear camera filming stuff, he was playing video games.

I really should have known he wasn't motivated enough, not even by his friend's death, to get out of those baggy shorts and Jurassic Park tee shirt.

The front door was unlocked, and I had walked right in.

I didn't see his mother on my way to the basement. She was probably somewhere getting him take out.

Skipping over the pleasantries of saying hello or a bright and chipper, 'hey', I stepped down the basement stairs and made my arrival announcement with, "You owe me two hundred, twenty-seven dollars and thirty-three cents."

Keith laughed. "For what?"

"My medication."

"Doesn't your insurance cover that?"

"I don't have insurance yet. It hasn't kicked in."

"When I get my check, I'll pay for it."

"When's that?" I asked.

"There's a sixty-day lag." Keith's fingers moved frantically in his game playing. "Don't worry I got you covered."

"Two months!" I shouted. "I'll be insane and what the hell check are you waiting on?" I plopped on the couch next to him. "You're a thirty-eight-year-old stoner without a job."

"I am working on my career," he replied. "My account is monetized. I'm getting like fifty-four bucks."

"That's hardly the two hundred you offered," I told him. "Get a job."

"I can't be tied down with a job. What if I have to go on a moment's notice to like an interview or something."

"You worked a job when you were trying to be a rock star."

"Yeah, and how'd that work out for me?"

"Keith, you'd be semi famous if you kept playing. You're good."

"Thanks."

"But you are far from an influencer," I said. "Rick is now an influencer, but he's dead."

"I know, right? How about his video going viral? And can you believe people are commenting that it's fake. A million subscribers."

"And you have sixteen subscribers."

"Um, no." Keith shook his head. "I'm up to three thousand now."

"What? How?"

"I did a Rick tribute video and showed pictures of us."

"Oh my God, that's so tacky."

"Your Baba said it was fine." He paused to grunt when he messed up in his game. "I asked her today before I did it."

"You talked to Baba today?"

"I saw her today. It's Wednesday. Bingo at the home. Remember? She loves when I go there, tells everyone I'm her famous grandson."

"Yeah, I am well aware. Unbelievable." I shook my head. "And you couldn't stop at the funeral home? You blew me off."

"You went?"

"Of course, I went," I snapped. "And, and ... Beyonce was there."

"Beyonce was there? You saw her."

"She was there, but way before me. I saw her name in the guest register."

"That is really cool."

"I know." I playfully backhanded him in the arm. "You didn't go."

"I couldn't, Harp. I couldn't go. Both Baba and my mom said—"

"Baba and your mom coddle you," I cut him off.

"Still. They said if I'm not comfortable don't go. Funerals are for the living, the dead don't mind."

"Oh, they mind," I replied. "Not sure Rick cared if you went or not. Wait... he probably does since he blames you."

Keith chuckled nervously. "Stop."

"He said it. Clear as day. His mom said you killed him. I said Rick doesn't blame you and Rick said, 'you don't think.'"

"You're joking,"

"I'm off my meds."

"Shit." The controller dropped from his hand.

SIX

BABA'S PEAS

"Faygo Red?" Keith stood at the open fridge door and reached in.

"Did your mom buy grape?"

"Yep." He handed me a can of soda.

"Thanks."

"Sit down."

I walked over to the kitchen table and had a seat. When Keith joined me, he not only had his Faygo Red soda, he carried a covered plate of sandwiches.

He lifted the plastic.

"What is that?" I asked.

"Sandwiches. My mom made them for me. Mustard?"

"No, I'm okay. You really need to stop making your mom do all this for you."

"I don't make her. She does it on her own. It gives her purpose, I guess. Now we're not talking about me. We're discussing you. So, it's been two months since you had your meds."

"Yeah, and I was doing fine. I just don't want to be crazy."

"I hate when you say that." Keith grabbed the mustard and added some to his sandwich.

"Say what?"

"Crazy. A lot of people struggle with mental illness. Not saying that you don't have problems. I mean the shit you went

24

through when you were a kid and the other stuff - it's bound to cause some long-term damage. Just don't use it so loosely."

"Wow, okay, that's kind of deep coming from you.":

"I can be deep. Anyhow, you took medication to keep everything at bay. But the medication wasn't your doing."

"At first no." I shook my head. "Then I just kept taking it because I didn't want that ability to come back."

"You never seemed scared of it," Keith said. "You were more scared of the idea of being possessed. You think you wanted it buried because of your mother?"

"Possibly."

"We never really talked about this," he said. "Only when you'd mention things here and there. So, this ability …you think it's back?"

"Yes, for sure," I replied. "I heard Rick."

"Did you?" he asked. "I'm not doubting you, I'm just asking if you're sure. Maybe it was someone else from the funeral home."

"That's possible."

"Was it only dead people?" Keith questioned. "Was that the only ability the medication suppressed."

"Well, the seeing dead people in my lucid dreams kind of took over the other abilities. Sort of like a step-up process."

"What did they want?" Keith asked.

"The dead people?" I shrugged. "I don't know. I never asked, if they started talking, I woke myself up. Which made me think at times it was all just dreams and not really dead people. The only one who really told me what he needed was my Uncle Earl."

"Oh, him, yeah." Keith shivered. "I remember in college us really researching that case."

"I was really curious and scared to look into it because when I was hit by that car and I saw him he swore he didn't do it."

"But he did," Keith said. "I mean, seriously, we read all that stuff. That was a pretty strong case against him. Maybe it was a dream."

"I was nine. I didn't know he did anything," I replied. "And I would believe it was a dream if I didn't pull him through the last time I saw him."

"I'm sorry, what? Pulled him through?"

I nodded. "Yeah, he grabbed my hand and when I woke up, I had pulled him through."

"From the other side? From the dream? Like the chick did with Freddy Kruger in that movie?"

Again, I nodded. "Yep, just like that. My mother even saw him. That's what actually started her plight to end me doing it."

"You never told me that part," Keith said. "Why?"

"I didn't want you to think I was crazy. I mean. You know what I mean."

"Dude." Keith dropped his sandwich. "That is some serious cool ability. Why would you want to bury it?"

"Why would I want it?"

"Maybe there's a reason you have it. Maybe there's something these people need to get out. Like your uncle. Maybe you're meant to do something with it. You should really think twice before shutting it down again if it's back. You're a lot older. It may not scare you as bad. But if you really want it buried again, I have almost three hundred available credit on my card." He lifted the sandwich again. "I can get your pills."

"Thank you." I grabbed his hand.

"Before you go back on those meds, you should really see if it's back. If it is, and you want to shut that door, I'll whip out the card."

"What about the funeral home?" I asked.

"We don't know if that was Rick. I mean, I don't know how you would test it, but I have an idea of a person you can talk to about it."

I was going to ask him who, then I realized who he meant.

Baba.

<><><><>

At ninety-four years old Baba was sharper than my mother was at seventy-four. While like most elders she repeated stories, it wasn't constant. Baba didn't miss a trick and rarely stumbled on a word. She attributed her sharp mind to daily reading, puzzle solving, and watching every murder mystery she could stream on her tablet.

Physically, she was a petite thing now. Her face was still full and youthful, but her body was tiny, unlike the thick woman I knew growing up. She moved quite well, used a cane for balance and was in the home because she didn't like living alone.

It wasn't a nursing home, more of an assisted living.

It was a nice place too.

Baba never left her room without make up and had her hair set every Friday.

When we arrived at the assisted living, the aids told me she was already in the dining room. Even though it was still a good forty-five minutes until supper.

She was the only one there and was reading a book while seated at the big round eight-seater by the kitchen doors.

I called out her name as we walked in.

She smiled wide and waved her hand high when she saw us.

"There's my famous grandson."

I looked at Keith and he shrugged with a snide grin.

"Hey, Baba." I kissed her on the cheek and grabbed her hand.

"Look at this. You have to come to see me again. Both of you," she said.

"What are you doing in here so early?" I sat down on one side of her, Keith on the other. "Dinner isn't for a while."

"Cream peas," she replied. "It's cream peas today. They never seem to make enough. If I sit in the back, I get served last and they run out of peas. I want creamed peas."

"Don't they have assigned seats?" I questioned.

"This is not high school little one. You know you can see the charge nurse and pay two dollars and stay for dinner."

"Dude," Keith said. "I love creamed peas."

Bubba reached over and squeezed his hand. "You can do a show on your channel. You're such a big celebrity now."

I rolled my eyes. "Okay, enough, no ego feeding. Baba, I actually came for a reason."

"Do you need money?" she asked and opened up the back of her book. "I have some ones I can—"

"No." I stopped her. "I don't need money. I ... Baba ... it's back."

She closed the book and stared at me. "You stopped taking those pills?"

"I couldn't afford them."

"Good. Good. You waste the gift washing it away with medication. Your mother made you believe it is a curse. It is not. So, it has returned?"

Keith clarified. "We don't know for sure."

"That's why I'm here," I said. "How can I find out for sure."

"Is there a way we can test it?" Keith questioned.

"The third eye just happened, it always did," Baba spoke gently. "The visits to the other side, perhaps practice the focusing again. Like you did as a child."

"Do you know if I focus on something in particular?" I asked. "Like does what I focus on, or where I am determine who I see."

"Little one," she squeezed my hand. "I was never allowed to help you. So, we did not test these abilities or what they mean. Only you can determine them now. Are you going to take the pills again?"

"I'm thinking about it?"

"Why?" Baba asked. "This gift is meant to help people, some way somehow. Again, all for you to figure out. Maybe it is time you truly learned the limitations of your gift before you limit and bury it again."

Even though she was saying the same thing as Keith, there was so much wisdom in Baba, that I would listen to her. I always did.

If I could help one person, truly help one person, then scared or not, skipping the medication for a little longer would be worth it.

SEVEN

FIRST TEST VISIT

"I'm pretty sure this isn't what Baba meant by helping someone," I told Keith as he escorted me in his mother's room.

"Sure, it is. It's helping me."

"Really, you don't count."

"I count. And." he pointed to the headgear camera on his head. "I will capture it all."

"What if it doesn't work?"

"It'll work."

"I'm not going to be able to do it with you staring at me."

"I'll be on the other side of the door. Call out if someone comes through," Keith said.

"This is your mother's room. It smells like Ben Gay."

"She has bad knees. Sit." He pointed to a chair.

I sat down.

"Look, we know from the past when you would do these trance things, you transported to another time or realm of the room you were in, correct?"

"Except with Uncle Earl. I don't know where I went to find him."

"Yeah, but didn't he tell you he was looking for you? Maybe whoever you run into today is looking for you."

"God, I hope not."

Keith laughed. "Or maybe the room has to have an association with the person."

"So, I should focus on someone when I try to trance out?"

"No. But …" Keith snapped his finger. "That is a really good idea to try later. Focusing on a person that died. In the meantime, just concentrate and focus on the Sleepy Time Kitty."

"The what?" I asked.

After walking to the dresser, he lifted a large, golden ceramic cat. I had seen one like it in a Chinese Restaurant. Only when he turned it on, not only did it wave, it made a soft white noise.

"Huh? Huh?" Keith shot a grin my way. "Good, right? My mother got it on eBay to help my dad sleep. He died in this room, maybe he'll visit you."

"Swell. Your dad was mean."

Keith laughed. "I know, right. Okay, I'll let you go. I'll be right outside the door, call me."

He stepped out, closing the door.

It wasn't going to work, there was no way. I hadn't done it on demand in decades, and even then, I never intentionally pulled someone through.

Maybe it was only Uncle Earl who had that ability.

I took a deep breath and relaxed, focusing on that waving arm of the cat and listening to the white noise.

I was fading, slipping into it, rather quickly, too.

"Ma, you can't go in there," Keith's voice snapped me out of it

"Why?" his mother asked.

"She's talking to dead people."

I cringed.

"Oh, okay, I see you're getting ready to film it. You are so ambitious," said his mother proudly.

"Thanks, Ma."

I moved my hand in a circle motion hoping they'd hurry it up.

"I'll let you go," his mother said. "Make sure you come get me if she gets a hold of your father, that bastard." Pause. "God rest his soul."

"I will."

"Did you want something to eat?"

"Um, yeah. In a bit. Hey, Ma, do you know how to make creamed peas?"

"Do I? Please. I make the best. I'll run to the store and get some stuff."

Finally, they were done. I heard her footsteps on the stairs.

I started focusing again.

I wasn't sure if it was the cat, the noise, but I slipped into it quickly.

Suddenly the room filled my ears with that blood rushing, underwater feel. The colors were muted some, but otherwise not much had changed. I looked left to right. No one was there. Slowly I stood from the chair and looked around the room. It wasn't that big. Perhaps I had been away from it for so long, that brightness I had about me, was now gone.

"Hey, Harp."

My eyes widened and I turned around.

Rick stood there. He was wearing a tee shirt and jeans. His hair styled in that rag top way.

"I have been following you since the funeral home. You have a light about you," he said.

"So I've been told. Why are you following me?"

"Aside from the light. There's something I need to say. Are you looking for me?" he asked.

"Yes. This is great. You have something to say, and Keith and I are trying something."

He shook his head. "I don't understand."

"You will. It's an experiment we need you for." I reached out and clutched his arm. "Wake up. Wake up, Harper."

Rick smiled, almost laughing at me.

The we crossed back. That fast.

I heaved out all the air from my lungs as my eyes popped open and I was awake.

I was still in the chair, not standing like I had been in the trance. Sitting there holding on to Rick. I had him. I had pulled him through. He looked like my uncle had. A slightly less colored, glowing three-dimensional image with auras of light around him.

"Keith," I called out. "You might want to get in here."

"Am I back?" Rick asked. "Am I alive again?"

"No, the light will come for you. You have to go back in it," I said.

"Sure. No problem. There's—"

The door burst open, and Keith stumbled in his shock, loudly, nearly tripping over things. "Shit. Oh, shit. Shit. He's—he's—he's here."

"She pulled me through like a Freddy Kruger movie," Rick commented.

"I know!" Keith said excited and nervous. "It's so wild."

"Dude, are you recording this?" Rick asked.

"I am."

"Sweet, that is so smart, make sure you tag it real life ghost encounters. You're gonna go viral."

"I know, right. We should set up an interview."

"Guys," I stopped them, waving my hands. "I don't know if he can come back, but look behind him. The light is coming."

"What happens if he doesn't go back?" Keith asked.

"We shouldn't find out." I faced Rick. "You said there was something you needed to say. Was it to your mom?"

"Yes," Rick answered. "I don't blame you, Keith. I blame Scotty. Because he was on that bridge with me. I wasn't supposed to fall in. That's why my phone survived the live stream, he caught it. He had a line on me. It was supposed to look like I fell and we were gonna tell people he saved me. The line snapped and I fell for real." Rick looked over his shoulder to the light that grew. "Man, I can feel that pulling. It's warm."

My mouth dropped open. "And this Scotty didn't call for help?"

"Nope. Someone watching the livestream did. He ran. He has my wallet and my last paycheck. I want my mom to have it. Hey, Harper, if you do this again, I don't think I have a choice but to go back. It's pulling me and I'm fighting."

"Dude," Keith said. "Thank you. I'll tell her and show her this. Okay?"

Rick nodded and looked at the camera. "I'm sorry, Mom. It was stupid. I love you."

And with that, Rick moved back slightly, then the light took him. It embraced him, covered him until he wasn't seen, and the light vanished.

It was completely silent for a moment.

"Harper, that was real."

"I know."

"I'll admit." He shook his head almost nervously. "That was a little scary."

"A little yeah, he said he was following me and had something to say."

"My heart." Keith laid his hand on his chest. "It's racing. That was incredible and …" he removed his headgear camera. "We have proof."

"We have more than that, something more important," I said. "We have answers for his mom."

EIGHT

UPLOAD

It was hard to see on the tiny screen of the headgear camera and Keith attached it to his laptop. In all the years I had known Keith, never did I see him bite his nails. But he chomped away during the file transfer. Like him, I thought the video didn't capture Rick. I couldn't see him and there was no audio.

However, once we viewed it on the laptop, Rick was clearly in the picture.

The video was weird. What was on the computer wasn't exactly what Keith or I saw. Clearly, Rick's image was there. You could make out his face and some features like his hair were really predominant. His clothes were not seen because he was a glowing image. The specks of light around him on video were like static.

His voice sounded almost muffled. The one thing that looked the same was that light that came in and took him.

"Oh my God, this is unreal." Keith paused the video. "I will have to do a video to introduce this."

"I guess. I mean it speaks for itself, can't you do a voice over or …"

"Hello!" his mother called out as she entered the house. "I went to the store." She walked into the kitchen where we were seated. "Got all the stuff for creamed peas. Thought I'd make some chicken. Are you staying, Harper?"

"Um, yeah, that sounds good, thank you Mrs. Levy."

She placed her bags on the counter. "How was ghost talking. Did you see Dad?"

"No," Keith turned the laptop to her. "Rick."

She looked, then quickly looked again. "Is that real?"

"Yes," I answered.

"Oh," she gasped out. "I thought that ability of yours was some crazy Catholic notion of your mothers to get closer to Father Mollohan. My goodness. Does he say anything?"

"Yeah, do you want to watch?" Keith asked.

"No. No." She waved out her hand. "Tell me what he said."

Keith told her. "It was an accident. He wasn't alone, he was supposed to set it up as fake. It went bad. Oh, and the super important thing. He's cool with me posting this on my channel."

"What?" I blasted him. "That's not the super cool thing. The super cool thing was he said he was sorry and loved his mother."

"Oh, Keith," his mother said. "You can't post that without showing his mother first."

"What if she won't even look?" Keith asked.

"You have to try," his mother replied. "If she refuses to talk to you or see, then post and it will make its way to her. But you do have to first try."

That was the plan all along. To show the video to Rick's mother first. Somehow it sounded like it was going to be easier said than done.

It was the day of the viewing, the funeral was the next day, we knew Rick's mother had to be exhausted. Like stalkers, we waited outside the home, watching people go in and out.

The poor woman probably needed a break.

I hated to do it, but if it were me, I'd want to know.

The grief she carried was unimaginable. Keith's mother even said Debbie needed to hear and see it.

Just to know your child was still in existence in some afterlife would be comforting.

We watched her pace the living room in front of the window, sipping from a mug. Keith had copied the file to his mother's iPad to easily show Rick's mother. After getting up the courage, we knocked on the door.

Really, what do you say? How were we to broach the conversation?

Excuse me, Rick's mother, we have a message from your dead son?

When she opened the door, her smile was tired, and then she saw Keith and whatever remained of that smile was gone.

"Go away," she said. "My son is gone because of you."

"Listen, Okay, I know you blame me." Keith tried to talk to her.

"I do."

"But Rick doesn't."

She laughed. "How do you even begin to think that? The last thing he said to me was if anything happened to him blame you."

"Oh, wow, that's not cool."

"Neither is abandoning my son." She started to close the door. Keith stopped her.

"Oh, that takes balls," she said. "I'll call the cops."

"That's fine. Just …" he held up the iPad. "Just watch the video."

"Of?"

"Rick."

"When?"

"Taken today."

"My son is dead," she said.

"And we have his ghost talking. He said—"

"You need to leave. Right now," she said. "I don't have time for this. This is a cruel joke."

"It's not a joke," Keith pleaded. "Harper, tell her."

"It's not a joke, Debbie, please watch it," I tried to convince her.

"I don't know what you two are up to, but I can't handle this. Leave before I call the police."

"Fine," Keith spoke quickly knowing his time was limited with her. "But call Scotty. He was there. He was with—"

The door slammed.

"Rick." Keith grunted in frustration. "She needs to see it."

"She will," I told him. "You tried."

"What now?"

"What now?" I shrugged. "Upload it."

NINE

LUNCH RUSH EARLY

The nighttime sniffling, sneezing, coughing so you can rest medicine did more than work just on the cold and the flu. It worked for me in a pinch so I wouldn't dream. Not that I had any strange dreams since going off the medication, I just didn't want to take a chance since the Rick interaction that it would all come back.

I wasn't ready.

When I left Keith, he was eating a bowl of creamed peas and getting ready to record his introductory video.

The last we texted, right after I took my double dose of green stuff, he was starting to edit.

I went to sleep and when I woke up, there was one text that came through at three am stating he was uploading.

Nothing since.

I had the lunch shift at the restaurant and had to be there at ten. I knew Keith was still asleep and I didn't bother to reach out. He would hit me up and give me a report on the video after he was awake.

He was expecting great things.

I wasn't.

My only hope was that it would make its way to Rick's mother.

I arrived at the chic Italian bistro in my black pants, vest, and crisp white shirt that I knew would be stained by the end of the lunch rush.

Everyone had to work a lunch shift if they wanted a profitable weekend shift.

There were three of us on, as opposed to a wait staff of six in the evenings.

It smelled so good in there with the tomato sauce and garlic. It was a great gig and the owners treated their staff well.

After clocking in, they announced the taster.

A new special the chef invented. Lobster mango ravioli in a sweet cream sauce. I wasn't sure how well that would pair up or even if I wanted to try it. But everyone had to taste it in case a customer asked.

It wasn't half bad.

We all did the back of the housework then moved to the front to get ready for lunch.

I was shocked. People were already lined up at the door. As I inspected water glasses, I could see them excitedly peeking in the windows.

"And here I thought Thursdays would be bad," I said to another server.

"They usually are," he replied.

"Looks like we might have to hustle today," Sergio, the owner said as he walked through the dining room. "A lot of people are waiting."

"Was there a good review or were we mentioned on the news?" I asked. "That's a lot of people."

"We're good."

I grumbled a 'hmm' and continued my work. Yes, the restaurant was good, but so good that people line up before eleven on a Thursday. I doubted it. I worked a lot of restaurants and the only time I saw this happen was when a Food Network Chef was doing a restaurant makeover show at the establishment I was working at.

Sergio walked to the doors to unlock them. "Big crowd; let's try to turn these tables over quickly. I'll have them move fast in the kitchen."

I moved near the bar with the other servers, waiting for my section to be seated.

Sergio unlocked the door.

He barely got a greeting out when the crowd just pushed in. They rushed the restaurant like concert goers to a stage, nearly knocking over Sergio.

It was chaos.

They bumped into tables, racing across the floor and I was mortified when they all ran to me.

They crowded me, shouting things. They pushed into me. Dozens of faces before me with shouting voices.

"My brother died, can you reach him?"

"My father has been missing."

"I need to speak to my sister. I can pay."

"Help me reach my husband …"

"The devil has his tentacles wrapped around you. Repent!"

Hands clasped tightly to my ears, I did the only thing I could think of. I ran.

Sergio's perfect hair stood on edge as he paced, scrolling through his tablet in his office where I hid.

He and the other staff managed to clear the restaurant, a few remained, promising they'd buy a meal.

I was frazzled. I wanted to ask what I had done, but I already knew.

I just found it hard to believe word go out so fast.

"Unbelievable," Sergio said and showed me the tablet. "Every news source is covering it."

I looked at the headlines of the article. "Hoax or afterlife."

"Oh my God." I closed my eyes. "How did they know it was me? How did they find me?"

"Well, Harper, it's easy. All they had to do was google your image from the video. Social media. Did you update your workplace?"

"Yeah."

"There you have it." He retrieved the tablet. "Everyone is an armchair detective. Information is everywhere. Is this real?"

"Yeah, yeah, it is."

"This article says that you were in the room with the ghost when Tar-Star Keith entered."

I slightly snickered. "Tar-Star Keith. Only he was outside waiting to come in. While I brought Rick."

"Brought him. I mean how did you get him to appear like this?"

"I have this gift, had it since I was a child," I replied. "I can go to the other side and pull them through."

"Pull them through?" he asked. "You yank them?"

"I'm in a meditative trance," I explained. "I hold on to them as I come out and they come through."

"Like Freddy Kruger?"

"Yep," I groaned. "Just like the movie."

"No wonder everyone is after you. You're gonna have people offering you large sums of money to see a loved one once more."

"Problem is Sergio, I don't know if I can control who I find or see. I always believed the choice wasn't mine, they found me."

"Just like those people out there. You may have to hide for a while until this blows over. Which won't take long."

"You think?"

"Oh, for sure," he said. "Two weeks. It'll be done. In the meantime, for today, I think you should go home."

"I need the money."

"And I need my business. I won't have it with all these people hammering to see you."

"Do I still have a job?" I asked.

"Yes, but for right now, lay low. Come back tomorrow, I'll keep you in the kitchen working."

"Thanks." My thank you was sincere. He was understanding and could have fired me.

I collected my things and as I grabbed my purse from my locker, I heard my phone. I lifted it out and saw the text from Keith.

"Are you okay?" he asked.

I replied. "Yes. You?"

"Yes. Can you come over?"

Before sneaking out the back door, I replied that I was on my way.

Keith probably woke up to this insanity. He needed me to come over. I could only guess he was as frazzled as I was over it all.

TEN

VIRAL

Getting out of the restaurant was easy. I left through the back door into an alley. But from there I had to walk the long way to find my car.

When I drove by the restaurant, so many people lined the sidewalks waiting to get in they never noticed that I had left.

It was insane.

The expression on Sergio's face told me enough, I didn't need to see the video or the headlines. I was just trying to figure out how it exploded overnight.

Sure, Keith had three thousand followers, but was it enough to create such a buzz that the news was picking it up.

What was it about the story that made everyone go crazy? I kept thinking it was the confirmation that at least in Rick's case, he didn't just disappear or die for good. He moved on, still existing, still having the same thoughts.

I never thought of how confirmation of an afterlife would mean to someone who suffered a great loss.

Any loss I suffered was before I knew the person.

When I arrived at Keith's, for some reason I expected tons of people to be there. After all, if they found me at the restaurant, surely, they'd find Keith.

But no one was there. Just his mother working on the front yard garden.

"Playing hooky from work?" Mrs. Levy asked.

"Something like that. Is Keith here?"

"Yes, he's inside with Saul."

"Saul? Who's Saul?"

"Oh, he's from temple. Very nice man. A lawyer."

I was hoping it wasn't another attempt to 'fix' me up, then when I heard lawyer, that made sense. Keith was preparing.

As soon as I walked into the home, Keith rushed to me.

"Harper, are you okay?"

"Yeah, I am, thank you. It's insane."

"Tell me about it."

"What?" I laughed. "No one is bombarding you, they crashed lunch rush at the restaurant and Sergio sent me home because of it."

"Yikes, sorry, but it's your face everyone is seeing. Not mine, and when I do show it, no one cares. I have however, got two hundred messages asking for interviews. Some paranormal science place wants to test you."

"No. They aren't testing me." I shook my head.

"Exactly, not when we can test it and show the world."

"Keith, no. No."

"Think of the people we can help." He grabbed my arms. "You have a gift; don't you want to help people?"

"I do, but I don't see you wanting to help people. I see you wanting the money."

Keith lifted his hands. "I'm not gonna lie. The sponsorship offers rolling in are amazing. I'll share the money. You know, since you lost your job."

"I didn't lose my job, I was sent home."

"Hmm. Yeah." Keith nodded. "You have to do this. You do. You let the gift come back and now you need to figure out why you were given it in the first place."

"Because I died."

Keith shook his head. "Baba said there's a reason. There is someone you have to help. I think we need to find that person."

"I don't know."

"Harper, we can't rely on the dead coming to you. They want you to reach out as much as those who came to the restaurant. Anyhow, we'll start. Anytime you want to stop, we'll stop."

"Fine."

"Saul's here," Keith said.

"The lawyer from your synagogue?"

"Yes, he reached out to me, and my mom is his friend."

"Well, it makes sense," I said. "He's a lawyer, he sees legal problems."

Keith winced. "That's not it. Come on."

I followed him down the hall to the small back bedroom where his mother did her crafts. When I stepped inside a man stood up.

On older man who looked tired. He held a picture frame in his arms.

"Thank you for doing this," he said.

"Doing what?" I asked. "What am I doing?"

"Harper." Keith turned me to face him. "The spirits come to you, right? Here's a test to see if you can find a spirit."

I glanced sideways at Keith as Saul held out the picture frame. "This is my wife, Lonnie."

"Oh, she's beautiful,"

"Yes, she was. She died six years ago. Just dropped dead in the grocery store," Saul explained. "I didn't get to say goodbye or find out if she was in pain. I need closure. And I have to ask her something."

"I understand. But I've never gone looking for a particular deceased person."

"Maybe," Keith said. "If you focus, and focus on her picture, she'll come to you."

"It may not work," I told them. "I may end up with Rick or worse, your dad."

"It's worth a shot, right?" Keith suggested. "I mean if this works, think about the people we can help."

I exhaled an exhausted, "Fine. Let me have the picture and the room. And that waving cat. Get me the cat."

Both Saul and Keith left. Keith returned shortly with the waving cat. I set that on the craft table next to the picture of Lonnie. In a chair not far from them, I focused, setting my intention on finding Saul's wife.

I wasn't sure what would happen, but I was about to find out.

ELEVEN

MOTHERS

Flying.

That was the best way I could describe the feeling. That or sitting at a traffic light and the car next to me moved, and I didn't, yet I felt like I was moving.

It was indescribable, really.

I watched that waving cat while staring intently at Lonnie's photograph. I knew as soon as I felt my soul moving, it was working. However, where it would take me, I still didn't know.

I moved out of that room, through the walls, and with a dream like feel to it all, the second I left the house, I was somewhere else.

Somewhere warm, sunny and beautiful.

I could see it, feel it and sense it

Like some sort of weird movie, I rapidly moved over fields of grain until I stopped cold at a tree.

A huge tree was in the middle and sitting on the ground, holding a book with one hand and a cup of something in the other was Lonnie.

It had to be her. Of course, she looked a lot younger than her photo, it was her. Her hair was brown, long and silk, a slender figure in a beautiful flowing dress.

"Lonnie," I called her name as I approached. My voice had almost a feedback, high tone to it.

She turned and looked at me and was startled. "A light person."

"Excuse me?"

"A light person, we were told you existed. People able to cross realms to the spiritual plane."

"I also have the ability to bring you back for like three minutes."

"Why would I do that?" she asked.

"Saul wants to speak to you."

She giggled then turned serious. "No. Thank you. I have nothing to say. He probably only wants to know where the insurance policy is."

"I have no idea what he wants. He says he misses you. Isn't there anyone you want to say something to? Your children? Did you have children?"

"I do."

"Then get a message to them. Let Saul see you and tell him what you want told."

Lonnie nodded. "Okay, fine. How does this work?"

"I'm going to hold your arm and within seconds, we'll be on the other side. You'll have about three minutes and the light will come for you."

"Alright. Give me a second to think of what I want to say." She closed her eyes and after a few seconds she opened them. "I'm ready."

I grabbed hold of her arm and instead of saying it, I thought it, 'Wake up, wake up.' If it didn't work, I could always say it out loud. But it did work and within a second, I was gasping outward, and we were in the craft room.

"What a cute craft room," Lonnie said. "Holy cow, I'm back."

"Saul," I called out. "Keith."

The door opened and they walked in.

"Yes!" Keith exclaimed in excitement.

"Dear Lord," Saul said in shock. "Lonnie."

"Hello, Saul."

"Thank you for coming back," Saul said.

"I didn't come back for you, Saul, I came back to say something to the kids."

"I understand. Lonnie, you died so fast. Did you suffer?"

"I don't know." She shook her head. "I was waiting at the deli and that was it. Saul, how are the children?"

"You can't see them?"

"There's not a looking glass mirror. No."

"They are good. They had a hard time. They're getting better."

"Tell them I think of them always," Lonnie said. "To be kind, and I love them."

"I will. Lonnie, I have to ask you something."

"I'm not telling you where the insurance policy is."

Saul shook his head. "No, not that. That's not important. I want your blessing to get married again. I want to know that you're okay with it."

Lonnie smiled. "Of course, I am, Saul. Live your life. Be happy, I am at peace and happy. Who is the woman?"

"Millie."

"Perfect," she said.

"Wait. Millie?" I asked. "Millie Levy?"

Saul nodded. "Yes."

"Wait! What!" Keith blasted. "You wanna marry my mom? You can't marry my mom. Stop."

"The light is here," Lonnie said gently, then looked at me. "Thank you for this."

Saul tried to touch her, but his hand went through, and Lonnie didn't wait for the light to take her, she stepped into it.

The light vanished and so did Lonnie.

Saul released a single sob.

"Hold on. Stop." Keith held up his hand. "My mom? When did all this happen? Where was I?"

"Keith," I scolded. "Quit. Okay?" I felt the vibration of my phone. "Shoot. Remind me next time to turn my phone off. It could have ruined everything." I pulled out the phone and looked.

It would have ruined everything.

A text message. My biggest fear.

It was from my mother. She found out.

TWELVE

UNKNOWN

'We need to talk now! And you know what it's about,' was my mother's text

I was firmly convinced no matter how old I got, there would always be that internal fear when having to face my mother after doing something she disapproved of.

A fear which was worse than being called to the principal's office.

My ride from Keith's over to my mom's proved I still feared my mother.

Now, I respected and loved her, but I also was scared of her. It didn't matter how young or old I was.

My father was just, well my father.

He was sitting in his chair working on a crossword puzzle when I walked in. He glanced up at me from the top of his glasses.

"Hi, Daddy."

"Harper," he said my name and accepted my kiss to his cheek. "What did you do to your mother?"

"Oh, good, she didn't tell you so she's not that mad."

"Huh?"

"Never mind. I'll be back." I kissed him again, then worried a little less.

Surely, if my mother was horribly mad, my father would know what I did. After all, there also weren't any extra cars, which means my mother hadn't called the entire diocese on me.

My mother was in the kitchen, I could hear her clanking things.

With my heart beating a little faster, I walked in. "Mom?"

"I made coffee." She held two cups. "Have a seat."

Thinking, 'Okay, she doesn't seem all that mad', I walked over to the kitchen table and sat down.

The coffee smelled really fresh and looked it, too. My mother joined me.

"I got up this morning," she said. "My knee wasn't hurting. I didn't have a headache. I felt good. Imagine my surprise when I opened my tablet to read the news and there you are."

"Excuse me? I'm front page?"

"Well, I had to scroll, but sure enough, the headline read, 'who is this woman with the gift. Real or fake.' That's what it said. With images that looked familiar to me."

"Mom …"

"What are you doing, Harper?"

"That wasn't supposed to happen," I explained. "Honestly, I didn't think anything would happen. I thought at the very least Keith's dad would show up."

"That's not a good thing."

"I know." I nodded. "He wasn't very nice." Lifting my mug, I took a sip of my coffee.

"That's not what I mean, Harper. This whole thing. This whole chasing after the other side thing. It's been decades. How is it happening? The medication was keeping it in check."

"I stopped taking the medication."

"You what? Why?" she asked.

"I couldn't afford it. I switched jobs and my insurance didn't kick in. It just came back."

"Of course, it did," my mother said. "You have to take the medication, Harper."

"No." I shook my head.

"Harper, I'll pay for it."

"No, Mom, no." I was adamant. "This gift—"

"Curse."

"No, it's a gift."

"Only if you can control it," she said.

"You never let me learn."

"That's because it controlled you and it had to be stopped. Uncle Earl for example."

"Was innocent."

"No, Harper." She shook his head. "No, he wasn't. He was guilty. Guilty beyond a reasonable doubt."

"Mom, he never got a chance to prove his innocence."

"Because there was no innocence to prove."

"If he was so bad, how was he in such a good place?" I asked. "How? Surely there's a place for bad people whether it's a hell or not."

"You think he was in a good place because that's what you were told to believe. Whatever force was behind it, it deceived you. Until you know to lift that veil of deception, you'll not see what it really is."

I laughed. "Mom, what are you talking about? Veil of deception? You talk like you're some sort of guru on this."

"You think your Baba is the only one who knows these things?" she questioned. "I had to learn. I had to learn it all to save you."

"Oh, that's right," I said sarcastically. "To save my damned soul."

My mother slowly closed her eyes. "You really think this is a religion-based thing?"

"Um, yeah, you sent me to all those places."

My mother grunted in frustration. "To save you. And … this is going nowhere." She stood. "I have to get your father to his eye appointment."

"Mom, I'm sorry, I don't want to argue with you, I don't."

"I know." She placed her hand on my shoulder. "I'm just worried, Harper. I can't go through this again. I can't watch you go through it again."

"Go through what?"

"Using this ability."

I glanced up at her curiously. Did she forget? I never had a chance to use my ability. She shut it down right away. Right after Uncle Earl.

She kissed me on the forehead. "I'll pay for the medication. Just let me know."

"Is there something you aren't telling me?"

There was pause to her voice when she answered me, "I have to go. Just, do me a favor. Think back. Just … think back. What are you missing?" Following another kiss, my mother left the kitchen.

I listened to her talk to my father, to get him moving for his eye appointment.

My mother seemed genuinely concerned and it went beyond some religious based reason.

Maybe it was my imagination. It felt like there was something she wasn't telling me.

She told me to think about what I was missing.

I had no idea what that meant, but I was curious and had to find out.

THIRTEEN

NOT YET ANSWERS

What was my mother not telling me? What did she mean about me 'missing' something?

Baba had to know, and while I hated to go and bother her, I knew that's what I had to do.

My mother hollered out for me to lock the door when I left, I said, "Okay."

I thought it was strange. One, she'd ask me over when she was leaving, and two ... so much unlike my mother, she would never just stop.

The 'I don't want to fight, let's just stop this now' attitude was so much unlike her.

She'd usually bicker and argue until she won.

So why did she quit?

Surely, my father's eye appointment wasn't so pressing that she would leave things up in the air with a 'lock the door' farewell.

Everything felt suspicious, like I was being set up.

I downed the rest of my coffee, stole one of those chocolate chip muffins she picked up from Sam's club and headed to the front door.

In my mind, my destination was to see Baba for answers about what my mother said.

But why not find out from my mother?

My hand was on the door. I locked it but didn't leave.

Slowly, I turned from the door and looked up the stairs.

My mother threw nothing away. She wasn't a hoarder, but she kept things in boxes from my life.

Heck, she framed my handprint picture from kindergarten.

She kept everything. She stored it in the attic.

Since she was taking my father to the eye doctor, it was the perfect time to snoop.

Was it right? Probably not.

Leaving my muffin on the key table, I walked up the stairs to the second floor and down the hall to the attic ceiling hatch. The string wasn't dangling so that told me she hadn't been up there for a while. The last one up there was my father because he always pushed back the pull string.

They kept a folded stepstool in the hallway for the purpose of getting to the attic. I unfolded it, climbed it and lowered the hatch.

One thing about my mother, she kept everything in boxes and would label them.

Harper age two. Harper first grade … and so on.

The last time I saw those boxes, I didn't pay much attention. It was just weird.

After ascending the ladder, I pulled the chair and turned on the light.

Christmas decorations to my right, old Tupperware, suitcases, boxes.

Not only did she have them neatly stacked, but she had also put them in order.

The last box was marked, 'Harper Adult—College plus

I guess I stopped producing memorabilia. Or at least I wasn't giving her enough to earn a box a year.

But prior to the adult box, she had one box for pretty much every year of my life.

I suppose inside were pictures, any awards, schoolwork or art projects I sucked at.

Stacked three high, from left to right spanned my life.

The first nine boxes were, Harper Baby to Harper Third Grade.

Then she started marking with my age.

It was odd because the switch from grade to age started with my accident. Perhaps because I missed so much school.

Harper—Ten to Eleven Years Old.

Harper—Twelve to Thirteen years old.

Harper—Fifteen to Sixteen years old.

Harper—Seventeen to Eighteen years old.

Stop.

Where was age fourteen?

For someone so meticulous it was strange. Surely, she wouldn't just forget a year.

Why would she hide the year fourteen box or was there even one?

I started looking around. Maybe it was out of order or lost. I spent a good fifteen minutes looking and there was no year fourteen.

Okay, stop and think.

Fourteen would have been ninth grade.

That was when my mother started sending me to special schools, hospitals, and churches.

As if my mind was a computer, I started scanning memories of the years. I remembered where I was after the Uncle Earl thing. All the priests, the churches. I remembered being on the tenth-grade volleyball team at Saint Agnes. Practicing for my driver's test in a golf cart at the psychiatric hospital at sixteen.

Graduating from Sisters of Saint Francis Convent …

For the life of me my ninth-grade year, age fourteen, was a blank.

Missing, like that box.

Was it my imagination? Was it really missing? Was it a mental block or was my mother spot on in telling me to think of what I was missing?

My day started normal, spiraled into craziness and, before it was even over, I was thrown into a mystery.

My mystery.

If indeed there was one, I was going to solve it.

Who would have thought, certainly not me, that I'd find my first clue leaving my mother's house.

FOURTEEN

LOST GIRL

Had I not forgotten to lock my mother's front door, I would never have seen it. I never looked behind me. But when I popped my head back in to reach for the lock, I saw my mother's computer.

She never used a screensaver, so her last action was right there on the screen. She never cleared anything or worried.

My father probably didn't think anything of it.

Oh, there goes Tina again, playing on that internet thing and using electronic mail.

Really, even though I was so far from the screen, I saw the big red fifteen percent off department store email open. Something told me to go over and look.

I was not sure what I was hoping to find, after all, my mother wouldn't be emailing someone about what I was missing.

Or would she.

As soon as I clicked out of that email and into her inbox, I saw the latest email wasn't the discount ad, it was one with my name as the subject heading.

The reply came from an AG Riddle.

I didn't read AG's first, I read my mother's.

Dear Father Riddle, it's been quite some time since everything happened with Harper. Both you and I were positive she would remain in remission from this thing. Unfortunately, news has come to my attention that Harper is not only having these experiences again, she appears to be promoting them. We both know how dangerous this can be. What can we do?

She attached a link.

Mystery solved. My mother was being religiously melodramatic again.

Shaking my head, not only at my mother but at myself for overthinking it, I clicked on the reply she received.

Dear Tina, as you know Harper is an adult and there is nothing you can do to intervene. Just be diligent, see if you can find out why it is happening and what you can do to stop it. If it progresses let me know immediately and we will get to work. What is buried should remained buried.

Okay, so my first thoughts were that he was just as crazy as my mother.

After seeking out that red discount email and bringing it to the forefront again, before I walked away from her computer, I opened another tab and for the heck of it did a search of Father AG Riddle.

He wasn't as old as I thought he would be. He was still an active priest. A pastor at a small church in Buffalo, and he also worked with Mercy Hospital. Both of which were twenty miles from our town of Aurora.

I didn't remember him, then again, I did recall my mother telling me several priests said I was fine. He was originally from Maine and that was all that was in there.

Nothing spectacular, no colorful background or mention of being an exorcist.

Confident that my mother was going overboard, and I was buying into her hysteria, I left my mother's house and locked the door.

My plan for the rest of the day was to just go home. I was tired, hungry and stressed. Since I had to drive through town anyhow, I'd stop at the sub shop, grab a sandwich and go back to my apartment.

No sooner did my phone connect to my car, Keith called.

"What's up?" I answered.

"Can you believe my mom is gonna get married? I'm just really thrown on this one," Keith said.

"I think it's nice. Maybe you'll finally move out."

"Um, no. Anyhow, what happened with your mom?"

"Same old. Same old. She was being all melodramatic. And check this out, I peeked at her email, and she even emailed some priest about me. Someone that knew me years ago."

"Probably one of those priests that she took you to," Keith said.

"That's what I think. It's insane, Keith. I mean, she had me second guessing myself."

"What do you mean?"

"I mean she had to take my dad to the eye doctor and did this cliffhanger thing to me saying, what am I missing?"

"What is she missing?"

"No, me," I replied frustrated. "She thinks I'm missing something."

"Like a religious aspect?" he asked.

"That might be it. My mind went immediately to like black out moments. Periods of time I was missing."

"Wow, that's wild. Why would you go there?"

"I don't know. I actually had myself convinced for a second, I couldn't remember my ninth-grade year when I was fourteen."

Silence.

"Keith, are you still there?"

"Yeah."

"Why didn't you say anything to that?"

"Because like …." He grunted. "That was the one year I remember we didn't talk. All my mom could find out was you were at a special hospital in Maine. None of my letters got to you and I never heard from you. I thought maybe you died and no one wanted to tell me."

"Are you sure? I don't remember being in a hospital in Maine."

"Positive. You can ask my mom," Keith told me. "Then again, that's what they told her. You may not remember because it wasn't true."

"You have a point."

"Harp, don't let your mom put all this shit in your head, okay? There's nothing wrong with you, nothing you don't remember and you're fine."

"Thank you," I said as I turned onto Main Street and hit town square. "I'm just tired. I'm gonna hang up, Sam's is up ahead, and I want to stop before I head home."

"Are you getting Sam's Subs?"

"Yes." I slowed down peering ahead.

"Can you get me a hot ham?"

"Keith," I whined. "I was going home. I wasn't going to your house."

"Come on, Harp, please. Just swing by and drop it off. You know I love Sam's."

"Fine. Fine. But I'm gonna go, I think I see a parking spot." After hanging up, I slowed down even more, eyeing that spot just before the light on the right.

It was a prime spot, and I was excited.

Knowing the car behind me was riding my bumper awfully close, I slowed to a crawl and put on my turn signal.

The light was green, and I expected the car behind me to zip around, I always hated pulling in and out of spots on the main street.

Four parking spots before the empty one. She was there.

A little girl in the middle of the road.

I was paying attention, I was going slow, still, I had to slam on the brakes. I came to a screeching halt, inches before hitting her.

She was no older than eight or nine and stood center of my front bumper, frozen there.

Her long brown hair looked unkempt and as soon as I saw her parochial school uniform was dirty, I not only worried that I had scared her from nearly hitting her, but something else was wrong.

I put the car in park.

The guy behind me beeped.

"Are you serious?" I asked, shaking my head. Clearly, he didn't see that I almost hit a child.

I got out of the car and walked around.

"Honey, I am so sorry," I told her.

The car behind me really laid on his horn.

Angrily I looked back and shouted. "Are you freaking serious right now!" I shook my head. "Unbelievable." Then I returned my focus to the girl. "I am so sorry. I didn't see you. Are you all right?"

Slowly she turned her head and looked at me.

"Are you all right?" I asked again. She had to have been in shock, scared out of her wits.

She pouted as if she were about to cry, then the tiniest voice seeped from her. "Help … me."

"Oh my God, you're hurt." I rushed to her.

She lifted her hand. My focus went immediately to the dried blood that was all over her dirty, tiny fingertips. She wept. "Help … me."

"Lady!" the man's voice shouted right near my ear.

I was so engrossed with the child, I jumped, peeped out a shriek, and looked at him.

"Are you gonna move this car or what?" he shouted angrily.

"Oh my God, you heartless bastard," I snapped. "Can't you see I almost hit her. She needs help."

"Who?" he asked.

"Her." I waved out my arm, pointed and turned.

"Who?" he repeated.

The little girl was gone. "She was just here," I said. "She must have run off." I looked left and right. "The little girl."

"Um, there was no little girl."

"You just didn't see her because she was small."

"Yeah, whatever." He backed up. "Move your car."

I nodded nervously and stepped back. I kept looking for her. She was nowhere in sight.

After getting back in my car, I immediately pulled into that spot.

Before I'd get my sub, I wanted to look for her.

There was something more going on than me almost hitting her. She was in some sort of trouble and asked me for help.

I had to help her.

FIFTEEN

SNEAK A NAP

"And you said about eight or nine years old?" Police Officer Lenzi asked me.

When I couldn't spot the child or see her running anywhere in the area, I immediately went to the police station. Surely, they could put someone on it right away. Even though our little police department had only eight officers, they were always on the ball, not to mention four of them were young and super fit.

Officer Lenzi was one of them. He looked like they pulled him out of some Marine Corp recruiting video.

"Miss Monroe? You said eight or nine?" he asked again.

"Oh. Sorry. Yes, she had to be about that," I replied. "Just guessing. I'm not really good on ages."

"And where did you see her?"

"By the light at Sam's Subs."

"I love that place." He paused in writing.

"Me, too. I almost hit her, she appeared out of nowhere when I was turning into my spot. When I asked if she was okay, she asked for help. She had blood on her hands."

"Blood."

"And dirt, yes. Then the man in the car behind started freaking out and the girl took off."

"And you didn't see which way she went?"

I shook my head. "She was scared. Really scared, and that man probably scared her even more. I think she was running from someone. I mean her hair was messy and her uniform was dirty."

"Uniform?" he asked. "What do you mean uniform?'

"Like a catholic or private school. A checkered jumper dress, white blouse."

"Nearest private school is in Buffalo." He stood. "I'm gonna put the word out. If she's running and scared, she may be hiding. We'll find her."

"Thank you." I stood as well.

"Miss Monroe, this is just a weird question. Do you think she was real?"

His question shocked me. "I'm not making it up or imagining it."

"I'm not saying you are." He lowered his voice. "I saw the video of you. Do you think this girl was ... real, in the sense of being a living person?"

Without hesitation I answered. "Yes. I'm sure she was."

He accepted my answer and moved on making calls to the other officers who were out on patrol.

I was certain the girl was real. After all, what reason would I have to believe otherwise? Yes, I communicated with the other side, but I never had a spirit come to me outside of meditation or a sleep. It just wasn't something that happened.

Sam's Subs was crowded but I got both my sandwich and Keith's. My plan was to just drop it off and go. I beeped the horn for him to come to the car. We ended up talking. I told him about the little girl and what the police officer suggested. Keith

71

dismissed it as well. And before he could start talking and my food got soggy, I took off.

Of course, it didn't end there.

He sent a series of text messages I read when I got home. How a major television station wanted to interview us and investigate. Keith didn't want to do that until we knew more.

We established I could just wait for someone to come or find them, but what would happen if several people waited? He was vetting the thousands of requests he received for help and promised only to choose ones that really did need it.

"Unlike Saul," he added. "Who just wants to marry my mom."

After agreeing to do another experiment only after I had a few days rest in between events, I finished my sandwich in peace, set my phone alarm for an hour and napped on the couch.

Even sleeping on the couch wasn't free from adventure.

Everything about my afternoon dream was normal. It didn't make sense, people looked odd. Fragments of my day were being dumped by my subconscious.

It wasn't a lucid dream, while it happened, I didn't know I was dreaming.

Sam's Subs was located in Luciano's, Sergio wasn't my manager, he was the vegetable topping guy in the sub line.

People were shouting they wanted free food, while Sergio insisted I wanted extra hot peppers.

When I said I didn't, he sent me to my room, pointing to a silver door.

Bam. I walked through the door like a pouting child and emerged into a room, instantly realizing it was a dream.

Just a room, gray walls like a basement. No windows. No people. I turned around to look at the door I have just came through and it was gone.

"Hello, Harper," he said.

I didn't recognize the voice. Why would I? It had been decades. But when I turned around, I knew him.

Uncle Earl.

He smiled. "I realize to you that it's been a long time. But to me it goes by in a flash. You turned the light on again."

"Not on purpose. I'm still debating on this."

"Why? Think of the souls you can help. Or better yet, the people they left behind."

"Did you call for me?" I asked. "Or is this a chance encounter?"

"I came looking for you and saw your light. I had to get by many people waiting."

"For me?"

He nodded. "Yes."

"I may go back on those pills yet. I can't do this every day. It makes my heart race and I'm pretty sure I stop breathing. Wow, wait, I should do a sleep study. Wouldn't that be interesting?"

"It could be."

"Yeah," I said with a thinking exhale. "Anyhow, I don't live with my mom or anyone for that matter. Pulling you through will be useless because there's like a three-minute window before the light comes."

He waved his hand back and forth to stop me. "I don't need to be pulled through and I'm sure I can't be pulled through again. It's like a one-time per person thing."

"Is that like written down somewhere?"

"It's just known. You're not the only light person," he said.

"I've heard."

"Harper, the reason I was looking for you is to ask, have you seen a little girl?"

In that lucid state I felt my heart beat faster. "What does she look like?"

"Long brown hair, wearing a school uniform."

Thump. Thump. I could feel my heart beat harder and my ears started to burn.

"Harper, I think she made it to your side somehow. She's looking for you. She could ruin … Harper, you're fading. Stay with me."

"Who is she?" I asked.

"Harper, she's …"

Gasp.

Snap.

I wheezed in heavily, grabbing my chest because it felt funny. As soon as I calmed, I jolted again when my phone alarm went off.

Reaching for it, I shut it off and sat back on the couch.

She was there.

The little girl in the dirty school uniform was standing in the middle of my living room.

She stared at me.

"Who are you?" I asked, blindly swiping my fingers on my phone to get to the camera. Lifting it slightly to do so.

"Help me," she replied lifting her hands.

They both had dried blood smeared on them, and she looked terrified.

As soon as I saw I had my camera open, I lifted the phone even more.

"How?" I asked. "How can I help you?"

"Help me."

I snapped a picture. No flash, nothing that would set her off. I wasn't even sure her image would photograph.

"Please tell me who you are so I can help," I pleaded.

She sobbed once. "Please find me."

Then, just like earlier at my car, she vanished.

Gone.

Hurriedly, I looked to my phone. While the image wasn't as clear as I saw in person, I did manage to capture her.

"Find you?" I stared at the picture. "What does that mean?"

SIXTEEN

IMAGING

Thankfully, Sergio had called me back into work that night as the salad prep girl and I stopped thinking about my encounter with the little girl.

A bad mixture of tequila and cold medicine knocked me into a dream free state.

I didn't get to tell Keith much at all. What I did convey was by text. I told him I was sucked into a lucid dream by my Uncle Earl who was looking for the same little girl I had almost hit with my car.

I think Keith was playing video games because he only replied with a 'cool'.

When I arrived at his house the next day, he was a bit more shocked.

"So, she's dead?" Keith looked at my phone and the image of the little girl. "Officer friendly was right."

"It was a good guess. And, since he suggested it, we may be able to get his help identifying her."

"Or, we take that news station up on their offer." He pointed to his computer screen. "We've been in constant contact."

I exhaled. "I don't want to go on national television until I perfect this. It could be embarrassing," I said.

"That's true."

"Can you negotiate with them?"

"Well … I sort of asked Saul to do that."

"Aw, that's so sweet, you're bonding with your future step-dad."

"Stop. Anyhow, did you need something else for me to negotiate?"

"Yes." I nodded. "I want to do a sleep study. I want to make sure I'm still breathing and not actually dying when this happens."

"That could have a lot to do with year fourteen. Maybe whatever it was, hit you really bad that year."

"Maybe. In that case the coma doesn't sound far off."

Keith handed me my phone. "First things first. Send that to me. I have a friend who is really great at photoshop. Let's see if he can bring out that image more." He lifted his phone and started to text. "I just asked him if he wants to work on a ghost picture for us."

"Sounds good. Should I send it email or text?"

"Email." The notification sound rang out and Keith checked his phone. "He said send it so he can work on it now." He swiveled some in his chair. "So why do you think Uncle Earl is so concerned about this little girl? It's obviously not the one he was accused of killing. We saw a picture of her."

"I ran it through my mind a lot on the way over here. Maybe it's a spiritual thing like, she made it through, and it shouldn't have happened."

"Do you think you opened a door?" Keith asked.

"Me or somebody else. There are others like me. Okay, it's sent."

"Dude, it wouldn't hurt to start searching for people who can do this, too." He faced the computer. "Maybe they don't know they can pull people through. Got your email. Let me get this picture to Lenny. See what he can do. And set up our quad."

"Our quad?"

"Yeah, I picked four people. For the group test. We'll schedule it for a couple days." His fingers clicked. "I'll get Saul on negotiating. In the meantime. Take something so you don't dream. We'll back away for a couple days and see if the girl shows up again."

"Yeah, she may only show up when I'm lit."

Keith looked over his shoulder at me and laughed. "Lit. Ha. Doing this drunk would be interesting."

"You know what I mean." I playfully smacked him. "Maybe the light I project dims when I am not active."

"We'll find out." Keith struck down with a dramatic hard click of a mouse. "Sent. Now we wait."

The Saul video racked up two million views in one day and over thirty thousand comments. Passing the time, waiting on Lenny, we read a bunch of those comments. Some of them were discouraging, some called me evil, a lot of disbelievers, but even more were congratulations to Keith on the marriage of his mom.

A viewer named Janagirl756 commented, *Ah that is love, he reached into the afterlife just to marry your mom.* Then she put some hash tag of '*True love exists*'.

It made me giggle.

Keith was not amused.

Finally, Lenny sent back the photo. I was impressed. While it looked more like something I'd see on a book cover, a slight combination of a photo and one of those highly impressive animations from a video game, it matched her.

Some details were off, but that wasn't Lenny's fault. He had her jumper uniform navy blue when it was green. Things like that he couldn't tell from the picture, because my phone picture didn't capture it.

Her face though was spot on and that was what I needed.

"He's gonna think you're nuts," Keith said when I told him I was headed to see Officer Lenzi. "And I don't use those terms lightly, you know that."

"He's the one that brought it up."

"Still."

"He's a cop. I'm willing to bet he'll be happy to know he was right."

Well, I was wrong on that one.

I waited forty minutes for him at the police station. I wasn't sure why I thought he would just be there. We didn't have that many police officers as it was.

When he saw me, Lenzi paused. "Yeah, I have nothing on the girl. Not yet."

"I do." I proudly held up my phone, showing him the picture Lenny had done.

"She's on a book cover?" he asked.

"What? No. I saw her. You were right. She was a ghost."

There were two officers in the station at that point. I didn't think either of them were paying attention until I said that, then they started making fun of Lenzi.

"Are you arresting ghosts now?" one chuckled.

"Are you turning into that lady from the YouTube video," the other said. "Shit. Sorry. That's you."

"Come on." Lenzi, ignoring the jokes, led me to a back office and closed the door. "Have a seat."

"Thank you."

"How do you have a picture? Artist rendition?"

"Sort of," I answered and swiped through my phone. "She came to me again." I handed it to him. "I took a picture and a friend of a friend tried to enhance it."

"Did she say anything?"

"Yeah, help me and find me."

"What does that mean?"

I shrugged. "I don't know. Maybe find her to help her get back into the light."

"This is crazy."

"I know, right."

"Is this uniform supposed to be green?" he asked.

"Yeah. How did you know?"

"Looking at the original … the crest on the chest of the jumper looks like it says Saint Catherine. My sister went there until they closed down." He handed me my phone. "In 1994." He lifted the lid to the laptop. "Maybe finding her doesn't mean her ghost. Maybe it means …" his fingers moved feverishly. "Finding where she is."

"Huh?" I was confused.

"I'm looking up something."

"In your police files?" I asked.

"No, on google," he replied. "I'm googling, unsolved missing girl Saint Catherine's."

"All that sophisticated police stuff, and you're using Google."

He produced a crooked smile as he glanced at me. "We're in Aurora."

"You really think Googling …"

"Ha. Bam. Found her." He turned the laptop to face me. "Is that her?"

"Oh my God." I looked at the school photo of the little girl. She was smiling, her hair perfect, and without a doubt it was my ghost girl. "That's her."

"Cherrie Tyrell. She went missing in September 1990. Never was found. Was on her way home from school. Eight years old."

"Why now? Why me?" I asked.

"If I read online correctly," Lenzi said. "You buried this gift for decades. Maybe she was just waiting for you to start again. So now I think we know what she wants. Peace maybe." He tilted his head. "She wants you to find her."

"Like her body?"

"Yeah. Maybe."

I sat back with a hard exhale and only one question.

How?

SEVENTEEN

OTHER PURPOSE

The alert tone of my phone reminded me to put it on silent. I was happy to be on the floor at the restaurant instead of making salads.

Thank God the intestinal flu hit half the staff. Not that I wanted them sick, I mean it was awful to hear. But Saturdays were big money days and Sergio didn't have a choice but to put me on the floor.

The message was from Officer Lenzi and he asked if I could go to the station before he was done with his shift at six. I told him I was working and that wouldn't be possible, I knew it was in regards to the little girl, Cherrie, and I needed to keep my head clear of it all for forty-eight hours. It had already been twenty-four, so I decided to meet him at the station in the afternoon. Plenty of time for me to finish that quad day with Keith,

The restaurant wasn't as busy as I thought it would be or hoped, but it was still steady, and I was on track for a good night.

"Harper," the hostess approached me. "I have that lone one top by the kitchen. It's not really in anyone's section. Do you want it?"

"Sure." I shrugged and looked at the one top. A single narrow table just on the outskirts of the hallway to the kitchen. At the table was a woman close to Baba's age. "We never sit anyone there."

"She wanted it. Said she was going to be here a while. I guess it takes her a long time to eat."

"Oh, okay."

I had four other tables that I actually just served, I'd be able to give the woman a good bit of attention, plus I would pass her a dozen times. I felt bad that she was alone, I wondered what her story was. Saturday night, she was the only solo diner.

I approached her. She was a beautiful petite woman, fragile, like Baba, weighing all of ninety pounds. She dressed very nicely. Her hair was short, white and silky. "Hi, welcome to Luciano's, I'm your server, Harper."

"Yes, you are." She smiled at me.

"Can I get you something to drink while you look over the menu?"

"I'll have that smoking old fashioned."

"Got it."

"And a shot of bourbon straight."

"Yes, ma'am." I turned to leave.

"Make that a double, I'm not driving."

I returned the smile. "You got it." I went over to the station and put in her drinks. I checked on my other tables, picked up her beverages and took them to her.

"Are you ready to order?" I asked as I set the drinks down.

She immediately picked up the double shot of bourbon and downed it like a champ. "I am now." She pushed the glass my way. "And you can bring me another."

"Double?"

"Yes."

"What can I get for you?"

I expected her to order the grilled chicken or something light. Instead, after choosing two appetizers, she ordered the Italian trio with an extra side of sausage and more bread.

She was so tiny; she was either taking it home or walking the bill.

The hostess was right, the woman was there a long time.

She took her time.

Two hours, four rounds later, not only was the woman still stone cold sober, there wasn't a speck of food left on her plates.

Everything was devoured.

While passing on dessert at the restaurant, she did order a slice of carrot cake to go.

I was dumbfounded. I couldn't believe it, in fact the entire staff was floored and wondering if she was dumping it in that purse of hers.

She just took her time, tiny bites, minding her own business, ordering the cake to go as we neared closing time.

The woman was one of the last customers remaining.

As I was bagging her cake, I printed her check, and the hostess approached me.

"Her ride is here. A huge limo."

"For real?" I asked.

"For real. Maybe the tip will be good."

"She was sweet and easy." I lifted her tab from the printer. "A shit load of food though."

I placed her bill in the holder and took that and the cake to her table. "I'll take that whenever you're ready."

"Give me a second." After opening the holder and peeking at the bill, she reached for her purse on the table. "Harper." She placed her hand on my wrist. "Do you know why I came here tonight?"

"To get an awesome meal." I joked.

"To see you." The woman opened her purse. "You are a light person."

For a second I wondered if she were real, but everyone saw her and I dismissed that she was like the little girl.

"Harper, stop now. You're young and beautiful. I noticed that you gave me the senior citizen discount."

"Yes, I did."

"I'm not a senior citizen. Far from it. I'm maybe fifteen years older than you."

I chuckled, she had to be joking.

Then I saw the seriousness on her face. She wasn't.

"I'm a light person, too. I was doing it since I was a child. I didn't bury it or stop. I'm not joking, Harper, look at me. This is what happens. It ages you. It ages you big time. My name is Mag." She set a wad of cash on the check holder. "My number's in there. Call me if you need me." She stood, grabbing her dessert bag. "Please stop. Stop now. If not for you. Do it before someone gets jumped."

Then Mag walked away.

She had me. She had me until that jumped thing.

What did someone getting attacked have to do with being a light person? I wanted to dismiss her as a drunk, rich old lady having fun at my expense.

However, something told me … she wasn't.

I felt a truth coming from my gluttonous and generous guest, but I didn't know what to make of it.

The tip was so generous, over a thousand dollars, that I shared it with the rest of the servers. They in turn were so grateful they invited me out for drinks.

We went to Stoney's, a little bar just on the last block of town. It was loud, country music and lot of people shooting pool.

There were at least six pool tables.

I got why the other staff invited me. I gave them money, but they didn't know me nor did they want much to do with me.

After arriving they kind of did their thing while I sat at the bar.

I planned on one drink then heading home.

"I come here all the time," the male voice said next to me. "I've never saw you."

Thinking it was a pickup, I prepared to tell him not interested and turned. I knew him. "Oh, hey, Officer Lenzi."

"Call me Ryan."

"Ryan." I nodded.

"Can I buy you a drink?"

"No, I'm good. Just one. I'm driving."

He gave a thumbs up. "Good. Mind if I sit?"

"No, please." I pointed to the stool next to me.

"You never come here?"

I shook my head. "I never go anywhere. Just not a social person. The gang from work invited me so I came. You?"

"Pool league. We just finished."

Another nod and I sipped my drink.

"Harper, I can't get this Cherrie thing out of my mind. Have you tried to do the ghost thing and call her?"

I shook my head. "No. I was taking a break. We have this quad thing tomorrow."

"Quad thing?"

"Yeah, Keith is inviting four people who need to speak to someone on the other side. We're gonna see who comes through. Like a test."

"Can I come?"

"Sure." I shrugged.

"Anyhow, now that I have you. Your uncle is Earl Easton, right?"

I paused in lifting my drink. "Yeah."

"Cherrie was suspected of being a victim of his. One of several girls that were missing."

I looked at Ryan. "I thought it was just one?"

"It was one. The only body found, and witnesses put him with that girl," Ryan said. "Unfortunately, he was beaten to death before his trial."

"I know."

"Anyhow, not to bring up the past. But you need to work on this Cherrie thing. Reach out to her, I think she wants you to find her body."

"I will."

"But that's not the reason I wanted to talk to you."

I looked at him. "What is it?"

"I have a case. A woman I went to high school with," he said. "Her daughter disappeared. She disappeared six months ago in Buffalo. She keeps looking. She is freaking devastated, and I just want to help."

"You think she is dead?"

He shivered an exhale. "I hate to say that. I do. The newest video, you went looking for a woman and found her."

"You want me to look for her?" I asked.

"Could you?"

"I don't know if I can. But I'll try." I lifted my drink. "Only if you come to the quad tomorrow."

"Really?"

I nodded.

"Deal." He held out his hand.

I shook it. "And bring a picture of the girl. The others are bringing photos as well."

"You got it."

I finished my beverage. "I'll take that drink after all."

Ryan signaled the bartender. There was something about him, his believing in me that felt good. It made me feel less crazy. He was a person in authority who didn't once question if what I did was real or not.

Maybe I would get answers for his friend.

I didn't know how the quad would go the next day, but I was certain someone would come through. Who that someone would be, remained to be seen.

EIGHTEEN

THE QUAD

One would think it was an elaborate Sunday brunch instead of a spiritual realm testing. Keith's mother said she saw it coming and in no way was she going to have people in her home and have them leave thinking she was a terrible hostess.

"It's not a party, Mom," Keith told her.

"Still, you have to feed people," she replied.

What was supposed to be just four people, plus me and Keith, ended up being more. Those four people brough a guest, of course, I invited Officer Lenzi, and Saul was there helping out.

He and Millie were so cute since they went public with their relationship. Keith was not as amused at their little displays of affection as I was.

Millie had out crab dip, mimosas, various fruit and salads, along with a brisket she had been cooking since early in the morning.

Everything was placed out in the dining room which was adjacent to the room we'd use to try to make contact.

A tiny room blocked not by a door, but rather a thick burgundy curtain. It looked like a covered window when I stood in the dining room. In all the years I knew Keith it was used for storage, unless they had a party, and then it was a coat room.

Now, everything was removed, and it was set up for me. A single reclining chair that faced a long table with the waving cat.

Everyone was to bring a picture of the loved one they wanted to make contact with. It wasn't to be big, just a small photo. We set them up on the table by the cat.

Five photos, which included the one Lenzi had brought.

I didn't want to know anything about their stories, nothing that would influence me or desire to reach a certain individual.

We wanted it to be open.

Along with Lenzi there was an older couple in their seventies, two women in their thirties, a teenage girl who was with a middle-aged man, and a couple in their fifties.

I told them all before I went into the tiny room, "I'll do my best, but whoever comes through, comes through."

After downing the second mimosa, I drew the curtain and stepped inside.

They were all waiting for my call, just outside the curtain, quiet and I guessed, anxious.

I looked at the pictures, all of them were men except the daughter of Officer Lenzi's friend. One man was older. The other three in their twenties. I started the cat and sat in the reclining chair.

It was comfortable and I instantly relaxed. Maybe it was the mimosas.

Okay, I said to myself, *Let's do this.*

Locked into the rhythmic sound of the waving cat, I slipped into a weird state right away. I called it weird because it was somewhere between a meditative state and sleep, like on an airplane.

I didn't move into the other side, as I did in my dreams, it encompassed me.

There were so many people staring at me, I looked at the faces for those in the pictures.

Two of the men from those photos, I actually spotted. The one in the baseball cap, the other in a blue windbreaker. I wanted to talk to them, make my choice. I didn't see Lenzi's friend's daughter anywhere.

I approached the two men from the photographs. I really looked for the third, the younger, bulkier built guy. I thought maybe he was behind me because there was a man's voice in my ear. "Pick me, I've been here longer."

"Are you here to pick one of us," the baseball cap man asked.

I nodded.

"Pick me," the man behind me said. "I've been here longer."

I'd get to him, I would. I faced the other men before me. "What is your name?" I asked.

"Jason," he replied. "Is it my mother? I think she needs to see me?"

"I want to see my mother," said the man behind me. "Pick me. I've been here longer."

"So, you've said," I snapped. I felt his hand rest on my shoulder, and I started to turn to tell him I would be with him in a second, when …

HONK!

A loud, obnoxious, road rage sounding horn blasted. It obviously came from outside. It was so loud and long it snapped me right back.

Too fast, I had a hard time catching my breath.

I thought I had failed and would need to do it again until I heard his voice.

"Thank you."

It was the same voice that was behind me. Obviously, he was still touching me when the horn blasted. I accidentally pulled him through. Slowly I shifted my eyes expecting to see one of the men from the photographs.

He wasn't.

In fact, he was nowhere near what I expected.

NINETEEN

ET TU BRUTE

"Thank you," he said, then slightly bowed his head. "I would like very much to speak with my mother."

My mouth opened and no words came out.

He wasn't kidding when he said he had waited a long time. I couldn't place a decade on him, let alone a century. His was a big man, tall and fit. Not professional wrestling muscular, but his arms were defined.

He wore shoulder armor, no shirt of course, and looked like a cross between a roman soldier and a gladiator.

Had it not been for the massive scars on his face, I would have one hundred percent believed he was an actor or had died going to a costume party.

Maybe that was the case. Surely, if he really was from thousands of years ago, he'd speak Latin and I wouldn't understand him.

"I don't think your mother is in the other room."

"Are you sure?" he asked.

"Yeah, I'm pretty positive none of them in there are here for you."

"Ask."

"Okay." I shrugged. "Is anyone in the other room waiting on a buff, half-dressed gladiator with a sword?"

In a split second, every single person from the dining room rushed in and crammed that little room.

I stood and cringed.

"Oh my God," said one woman.

"This is real," Lenzi said.

"Dude," Keith gushed. "Cool."

"No, it's not." I shook my head. "He came through by accident."

"No," Gladiator man scoffed. "It was intentional. My mother is not here."

"No shit she's not here," I replied.

"Perhaps she is in the village."

"She's not in the village," I said. "There is no village."

"Did they destroy it?"

"No!"

"Can you help me find her?" he asked.

"No, I can't, sorry," I told him. "You shouldn't have come through without my permission."

"You brought me."

"You touched me," I said. "And …there's not enough time, the light is coming."

"For?" he asked.

"You."

"What does that mean?"

"It means …" I pointed behind him. "You have about one more minute before it takes you."

"Takes me where?"

"Back."

"No, I am not ready."

"You don't have a choice," I said. "It will take you."

"It will not."

"It will."

"Not if I run from it."

I watched the light grow bigger, reaching for him.

"The pull is great," he said bravely. "But I have faced greater threats."

With a laugh, I nodded. "Yeah, you're not running from it."

"Watch me."

I laughed again and then he ran. He ran right through everyone and the curtain. The light grew enormous, taking up the entire wall and then, it sucked away. It disappeared as it did before, only he wasn't wrapped in it.

We all stood there.

Keith looked left and right. "Did he get sucked in remotely."

Millie pointed to the curtain. "He ran. Maybe it got him on the other side of the curtain."

I was the first to rush out and see.

He wasn't in the dining room. It was that moment I believed that Millie guessed right.

The light came at him from another angle.

Until I heard one of our quad guests gasp, "Oh shit, he's still here."

Before I could mutter out 'where' I saw him.

He was by the front door. While still ghost like he wasn't nearly as translucent, and the rays of light no longer surrounded him. He looked even more like a thicker holograph.

He'd run forward to the door, bounced back, stared at it and tried again, repeating it until he saw me.

Then he stopped.

"There is an invisible force that will not let me through," he said.

"Is he stuck in my house?" Millie asked. "He can't leave?"

Gladiator man stood straight, extended his chest. "I will keep trying."

"You do that," I told him.

He returned immediately to his 'cat chasing tail' routine of trying that door.

Officer Lenzi shifted his eyes from the persistent soul then to me. "What do we do now?"

I didn't answer because I didn't know. I honestly didn't know.

The elegant black business card with the embossed gold lettering spelling 'Mag' was nestled in the stack of hundreds and twenties she had left on my table at the restaurant. I grabbed it knowing one day I would need it. I didn't think it would be the next day.

It was like getting through to the president calling her. Twenty minutes later, I was connected. She didn't have time to talk because she was about to board a plane. But she answered my questions and invited me over when she returned from Paris to discuss more.

"So?" Keith asked. "That conversation was brief."

"Yes, it was. She invited me over when she gets back from vacation."

"What did she say."

"He's stuck here."

"In my house?" Keith asked, almost panicked. "Wait. Why am I worrying about this? Think of the views I'll get."

"Don't get too excited. The light will come again for him." I looked beyond Keith to see our gladiator guy running for the door. I walked over to him. "You can stop that now. You're not getting out of here."

He faced me. "How will I find my mother?"

"Um, you're not. Not on this side of things, especially not now, so, come away from the door. We might as well find out about you while you're here."

I told Jason's mother about seeing Jason on the other side with the promise I would seek him again and then we politely asked them all to leave.

Millie felt bad and made little to go containers for them, they really did want to stay, but I thought it was too much on the new guest and me.

Officer Lenzi stayed, and we sat at the table.

Our unexpected guest kept pacing back and forth in front of the buffet table.

"When's the light supposed to come?" Keith whispered.

"Mag said it will come once a day.' I glanced at our gladiator guy. "We really want to know about you."

"This …" he pointed to the food. "Is a bountiful and magnificent feast. Who prepared such a meal?"

Millie giggled like a schoolgirl and walked to him. "That would be me."

"Ah, woman, my own mother." He touched his heart. "Was a cook, that is how I knew her. Fond story of mine. She took employ as a cook to be near me. Mothers in those days did not see their boys after six years of age."

Saul who had been quiet, spoke up. "When exactly are you from?"

"I am not familiar with a when I am from, I can tell you where I hail."

"Okay where?" Saul asked.

"Sparta."

"Oh!" Millie chimed excitedly. "Like Russel Crowe in Spartacus. You look and are built just like him."

Keith snorted a laugh. "No, he is not. Maybe built like Russel Crowe when he stopped working out."

"Who is this bird man?" the gladiator guy asked.

Keith waved out his hand. "No worries. You're not him. Russel Crowe didn't play Spartacus he played Maximus. A gladiator."

Our guest gasped. "A gladiator I am not."

"Yeah, now being from Sparta means you're a warrior," Keith explained to us then stood. "Think of the movie Three Hundred with Gerard Butler." He walked over to the buffet table. "I'm a history buff. I know the Spartan Army spanned hundreds of years. Were you familiar with Leonidas?"

"He is a great warrior and leader," he replied.

"What is your name?"

"Galen." He nodded and struck his heart.

"I'm Keith, and the cook here is my mother, Millie. That's Harper." he pointed. "She brought you through. Officer Ryan Lenzi. He's an officer of the law, but not in uniform right now. You can relate. Also, Saul," he said begrudgingly. "And you my new friend are more than two thousand years in the future."

Galen turned quickly. "Two thousand years?"

Keith nodded.

"That is why the surroundings look unfamiliar. I have been dead for two thousand years."

"Yep."

"No wonder my mother is not here."

Keith laughed. "Yeah, she's not here. But hey, I'd like to put you on my show while you are here. I mean I am a social influencer. Not sure you know what that is."

"I do," Galen answered proudly. "We had several social influencers. They would walk the streets informing people of wonderous new things. I would gladly be on this ... show."

I interjected. "You're gonna have to make it fast. The light will come back for you. It will come back tomorrow.:

"I will run from it," said Galen.

"It will come back."

"I will run again."

"Why?" I asked and stood as well. "Why? There is absolutely nothing on this side for you. No one you need to see. You cannot stay here forever. Okay, maybe you can, I don't know. But why won't you go back?"

"I am a warrior," Galen replied. "One of my greatest gifts was to sense danger and know that I will be needed. There is danger coming. I will be here to help. To stop it."

His response made me chuckle sarcastically. "Not sure if you realize this, but you are not in a human physical form. As noble and gallant as that is, I don't think there's anyway you can help."

He smiled arrogantly at me. "You never know." He placed his hands behind his back and looked around. "I think I will explore this castle."

"Oh." Millie jumped forward. "Come, I'll give you the tour."

I watched as Millie and Saul walked away with the spirit.

"Dude." Keith faced me. "Why are you so mean to him?"

"Not mean," I said defeated. "He wasn't supposed to come through."

Lenzi got up from his seat at the table and walked over to me and Keith. "Maybe, you know, there was a reason. Maybe fate put him in the path to come back here. You heard him, he feels danger."

"Stop. Seriously?" I shook my head. "You can't possibly believe that."

"Harp," Keith said. "You've seen movies. Ghostbusters. Key master, gate keeper shit."

"Bad things," Lenzi interjected. "Do come through. You of all people know that, right. You lived it."

His words brought pause to me and curiosity. "What are you talking about, Ryan?"

He laughed nervously. "You're kidding, right? I heard the story from my parents. They were friends with yours. Unless it's not true and ..." he slowed down his words, moving his eyes from Keith to me. "You don't know."

"Know what?"

"What they say happened when you were a teenager?"

"When I was fourteen?" I asked.

"Yeah. So, you do remember?"

"Nope." I shook my head. "But it's time to find out."

TWENTY

SECRETS UNBOUND

Officer Lenzi offered to tell me what he knew. I declined. We'd compare notes later, after I heard it from what I believed was the horse's mouth—my mother.

Unless someone has no respect or love for their mother, no one wants to confront the woman who gave birth to them.

I certainly didn't.

I loved my mother, but there was a fear about going up against her. It wasn't that I wanted to do it, I just wanted her to cut the bull and tell me the truth.

I hated leaving Galen at the Levy house without me. They were treating him like a long lost relative and I could see the wheel spinning in Keith's mind on how he could make money off of him.

Galen wouldn't be gone when I returned. He would avoid the light, he seemed hellbent on that.

After leaving Keith's I made a beeline for my mother's house. My father was in the living room, doing his normal thing of playing on his tablet.

"Hey, Dad, where's Mom?" I asked, kissing him on the cheek.

He didn't look up. "In the kitchen. Rolling meatballs."

"Thanks."

"Everything okay?" he asked.

"Yes. Thank you."

I went into the kitchen, where sure enough my mother was making her Sunday meatballs.

"Harper, you're early for dinner."

"I'm not here for dinner, I'm here for answers."

"Okay."

I pulled out a chair at the kitchen table and sat down. "You said to me it was what I was missing. I am missing my fourteenth year."

My mother immediately stopped cheerfully making meatballs, turned on the sink, washed her hand and dried them with a towel.

"What happened, Mom? What is it that Officer Lenzi knows, and I don't?"

"Oh." She grunted and joined me at the table. "That Genevieve Lenzi has a big mouth."

"It doesn't matter. What happened?"

"I expected you to remember at some point. But it never came back to you and I thought it best since you were taking medication to not tell you."

"Why?"

"Because it's not good, Harper. What happened to you, what we did to stop it."

"Mom."

She folded her hands and closed her eyes for a second. "Harper, when it happened with Uncle Earl, after that, it seemed as if, intentional or not, it was happening all the time."

"It wasn't intentional. I didn't know how to control it. You wouldn't let anyone help me," I said.

"Because it was a bad thing."

"And all of that was before Uncle Earl, after him, nothing happened."

"You don't think?" she asked. "It did. This is why you need to stop. Stop now."

"I can help people. I never learned how to control it. I'm learning now."

"At what cost?" she asked.

"That's what I am trying to find out. What price did I pay before?'

"Your soul."

I looked at her serious then laughed. "Mom, stop, that's so melodramatic."

"I'm not joking, Harper. Father Riddle has an entire box of files of the events. He's holding on to it."

"So, you had me exorcised."

"Don't be ridiculous you weren't possessed by a demon or the devil."

"Oh, of course. But you went to a priest first?" I asked. "Right?"

"I went to the Diocese, and Father Riddle was the one that got in touch with Doctor Hayward in Maine. A medical research institute and that doctor ran the unexplained department, they called it back then. Hayward is still alive; he oversees things in that department now. I called him."

"I'm so confused." I shook my head.

"Well, it's gonna be a lot to take in." My mother stood, walked to the sink and reached down inside. "Would you like a drink?" she held up a bottle of brandy.

"Yeah, please."

She poured me some brandy and then rejoined me at the table. "As I was saying, after you brought Earl through, things started happening. You were going to the other side more and more."

"Was I bringing them back like with Uncle Earl."

"We know for sure of one other time. It started affecting your sleep, your schoolwork. At first, we thought it was because we moved you to a private school and then ... and then you changed."

"What do you mean?"

"You changed. You were no longer you. We don't know who you were. The being inside of you was dark and bad. It killed things."

"I killed things?" I asked. "Oh my God."

"*You* didn't kill them. He did. He tried to pretend he was you, when you started fighting, doing things to other girls in school, mean things, we suspected. When we found the cat in the freezer, we knew it wasn't you. Something had gotten into you."

"Something?"

"A being. A damned soul. It wasn't like the devil because we went to the church you were fine in there. You looked like hell. You were no longer in there, Harper. After a few weeks, we took you to the institute in Maine. I truly believe had we waited longer, people would have died. The being was that sick and twisted. You were safe in the Institute. During a simple CT scan, they caught something on the imagery. An image of a man. It happened only once."

"You say you have a file on me?"

She nodded. "Complete with pictures."

"How did it end?"

"Not well. Finding someone wasn't as easy as going on the Internet. It was still new. But Doctor Hayward found a woman only because his brother was a general and she had done some work for the government. I don't know what it was." My mother waved her hand. "I don't care. She helped out. And it was something I will never forget. We almost lost you, Harper."

"What happened?"

"This woman was only about fifteen years older than you, but she looked much older."

"Was it Mag?"

My mother's eyes widened. "You know her."

"She came to the restaurant and told me to stop."

My mother made this relief gush. "She kept her promise. She said she would stay close and keep an eye out."

"Mom, what …"

"Your soul was gone, Harper, gone. To the other side, dancing around in some step-down heaven, I guess. The only way to get you back was to kill your body. It was a gamble but one we had to take. We had three minutes. We medically stopped your heart and killed you. The being was ejected at the moment of your death and within seconds that light appeared and took him. Then as the doctors worked to bring you back, Mag went to the other side and found your soul. She pulled you through. When your heart started, you were able to jump back in your body."

"I understand why I don't remember this, but a whole year is missing," I said.

"It's because you were in a coma for a while. You came back. You were in the hospital until they figured out what medications would stop it. This is why you have to stop and not do this. Bad things can happen."

"I understand." I nodded and sipped my brandy. "I do and I will. I promise. I'll stop. But I can't yet. There are things I kind of did, unintentionally mind you, that need to be resolved first."

"What are you talking about."

"Don't worry, I also have been in touch with Mag."

"Harper."

My father laughed as he walked into the kitchen with his tablet. He walked blindly looking at it. "Oh, Harper you have to tell me how Keith does these special effects." He shook his head and sat at the table. "The Spartan Warrior is hysterical. How did he make him look so ghostly? This is great. Who's the actor? Is he local?"

I looked at my mother.

"I get it. Trade secrets. Why did you stop making the meatballs?" my father asked my mother.

"Harper's fault," she replied. "She just held me up wanting her booze." My mother stood, looked at me in that scolding way and whispered. "Stop this now."

I nodded and scooted to my father looking at the tablet.

There were seventeen thousand views already on Keith's live video entitled, 'Ghost of Spartan Warrior Talks About His Life.'

I wasn't exactly honest with my mother. Galen wasn't the only thing I had to resolve. I promised Ryan Lenzi I'd help him and there was still the matter of the little ghost girl running amuck.

TWENTY-ONE

TO KNOW GALEN IS TO LOVE HIM

When I left my mother's. I had at least twelve text messages from an impatient Officer Ryan Lenzi. One would think he had a life or a mother to visit on a Sunday. Before driving off, I called him. A conversation that took fifteen minutes outside my parents' house.

I wasn't sure what to expect when I returned to Keith's house. Last I knew he was interviewing Galen about historical figures. Knowing Keith, he was probably recording episodes to show after Galen returned.

I didn't knock, I usually didn't. When I opened door, I heard laughter coming from the dining room. Then I heard Galen.

"He went down the same path. We had said stop, but that Artemis insisted the short path was valid and safe, and he tumbled down as well." He laughed at his own story. "Many of our warriors laughed with their souls that day I can tell you."

"What about the Jews?" Millie asked. "Historically, I am curious. Did you get along with them?"

"Yes. As our King Aerus once said, we are sons of Abraham, brothers to the Jews."

"Isn't that nice to know."

I stepped into the dining room.

"Aw," said Galen. "She has returned from her information quest."

Keith asked. "How did it go?"

"In a nutshell, short version, when I was fourteen, I was possessed, not by a demon, but by a murderer who jumped in my body when I pulled him through. On a positive note … Mag actually helped me then."

"Jumped in you?" Keith asked. "Whoa, kinda now makes sense when Mag mentioned being jumped.'

"Here we thought she meant a mugging."

"Rest assured, my fair woman," Galen said. "While I am here, I will stand guard in your slumber. No one will enter your body in my presence."

With a little laugh, I sat down. "Thank you. Did I miss the story of Galen?"

Keith shook his head. "Nope we were waiting on you. You brought him. You get the honors."

"Oh, cool." I glanced up at Galen. "Were you married?"

"You mean did I have a wife?" He shook his head. "No, we have no time to find love. Once we retire then we can. I was two years from that and enjoying my own offspring."

"If you had a son and it was tiny, did they kill it?"

"What!" he blasted shocked. "Kill an innocent baby? Where did you hear this?"

"From the movie *300*."

"Three hundred what?" he asked.

"Soldiers led by Leonidas."

"Three hundred soldiers led by Leonidas all told you small babies are killed?"

I waved my hand. "No, no, no. It's a movie. A movie is like a performance, a play on a painting that moves, and you can watch it any time."

"Is it always the same?" he asked.

"Yes, it is. Next question," I said. "Why were you looking for your mother so desperately? I get it, it's your mother, but is there something important you needed to say?"

"Yes," Galen answered humbly. "I just needed to make sure she knew the truth about me and my death. She could have been told incorrectly."

"How did you die?"

"I was betrayed. An enemy was amongst us."

"So, you didn't die in battle?" I asked.

Galen gasped so loudly in shock you would have thought I said something offensive. And I had no idea spirits could gasp. "Woman, I did not die in battle. I told you I was betrayed. I never saw it coming. I was sitting with my men, talking, laughing, enjoying wine, when it occurred. I went from smiling to looking down and seeing the sword coming from my chest."

"Dude," Keith snapped. "You were stabbed in the back? That was so wrong."

"Yes, it was," Galen said. "I just want my mother to know I did not betray anyone and I was not a coward."

"Maybe they told her you died in battle," I said.

"Woman!" Galen scolded. "I am much too good of a warrior to die in battle. One does not die on the battlefield. One walks off and dies."

I stifled my laugh. "Why are you so offended? I thought it was the greatest honor to die on the battlefield?"

"If a warrior dies on the battlefield, how does one know he feels honor," Galen said. "The greatest honor is to go home victorious. These lies. Do they come from that moving picture?"

I nodded. "They do."

Galen faced Millie. "Cook. You are resourceful, can you find me this moving picture so I can correct these errors?"

"Oh my." Millie jumped up. "Yes. I love that movie. Come on, we'll watch it on the big screen."

Keith turned to me. "Guess we're watching *300*."

It was probably the best news I heard all day. To watch the movie with someone that not only never saw a movie, but lived that point in history, was interesting.

More than the intrigue over the movie, I was intrigued when Galen said he would stand guard while I slept.

After the revelation of my past, maybe having a warrior at my side wasn't a bad thing after all.

TWENTY-TWO

DIG DEEP

The last time I slept over at Keith's we had both gotten drunk playing a video game. I wasn't drunk, but knowing I had to get up in the morning for work and Galen had vowed his protection, I stayed over.

Without sleep aids, I slept, and I didn't dream.

Nothing got through and I went nowhere. It felt good and I was rested.

Millie had breakfast for me, which was exciting. I couldn't recall the last time someone made me breakfast.

The night before was fun and it was eventful watching 300 with Galen. He kept commenting on the bodies of the actors, how they had a disease because they had lumps on their abdomens.

Then we showed him Star Wars, which ended up turning into a four-hour movie.

Galen stood guard at the foot of the bed. He was there when I went to sleep and there when I woke.

I didn't feel restless or rattled.

It was going to be a good day.

I had a ten-hour shift ahead of me. Lack of employees available and Mondays were always busy. It was a family style, meal deal.

During the lunch rush businesses would come in to get the platters of food and families flocked in at night.

I was on the ball. Even Sergio commented how focused I was. We should have knocked on wood.

The only issues I had was the weight of the heavy family style platters.

"Penne up, meatballs, sausage, table ten, Harper," the cook called out.

"Got it." I reached for the line, grabbing platters and placing them on the tray.

"Hey, Harp," another server approached. "Can you drop a serving spoon off at table eight?" She extended the large metal spoon that looked like a large spork.

"Sure." I took it, placed it in the front pocket of my apron, then hoisted my tray above my left shoulder. Rear end first, I went through the swinging door and carried the food to table ten. I figured I'd drop it first then leave the serving spoon for table eight.

I grabbed the tray holder, unfolded it, and balanced my tray upon it.

Just as I lifted the pasta, I saw her.

The little ghost girl, Cherrie. She stood outside the restaurant by the window looking in, and she wasn't alone.

Two other little girls were with her. They stood at either side of her. One wore jeans and a tee shirt, she was slightly taller than Cherrie. The other was smaller and younger, a tiny little thing, wearing a dirty yellow sundress. All three looked disheveled, hair matted, blood on their hands.

The tiniest of them, the girl in the sundress, lifted a fist and Cherrie waved for me to come out.

"Could we have red pepper flakes?" someone at the table asked.

"Um … yes, sure," I replied, staring out the windows. I placed down the third platter, didn't fold the tray holder and just walked out.

I don't know what possessed me, what caused me to do so. But the trio of little ghost girls called to me. The moment I stepped outside, Cherrie waved again.

"Find us," she said and walked away.

I followed.

I must have looked mad, in some sort of psychotic trance. I followed them.

I heard my name being called as I crossed the street.

"Harper, where are you going? What are you doing?"

But I just kept walking.

We crossed the main street, through the small park, then to a residential street.

They kept walking, looking back at me occasionally, and I kept following them.

At the end of the residential street was a truck garage, we passed through that parking lot to the main road. There was a secondary highway.

Horns beeped, tires screeched, as I walked entranced and haphazardly across the busy road.

The three of them passed through the guardrail. I climbed over, walking down the grade. I had no idea where we were going.

There was an old junkyard at the bottom of the small grade. We didn't stop there. I turned left down a small alley way and at the end was a parking lot.

The concrete was cracked and overgrown, beyond it was an old church. A small wooden one, boarded up and long forgotten.

Yellow tape crossed the windows and a construction fence surrounded it.

Not far from that church was an abandoned playground. A rusted swing set with no swings, a slide and monkey bars.

The three girls moved through that to the tree lined area. It looked more so decades overgrown than a forest.

The girls stopped.

The tiny little one held up her fist again, while the taller girl in jeans pointed down.

"Find us," said Cherrie. "Here."

I looked around. I was surrounded by trees and brush.

"Dig," said the taller girl. "Dig"

"Here?" I asked.

"Dig."

All three chanted the word eerily. "Dig. Dig."

As if I were possessed again, I dropped to my knees. At first, I used my fingers and then I remembered the serving spoon in my apron, I pulled it out and just started to use that.

It was maddening. The feeling that I had to remove the soil was overwhelming. I dug deep, spoonful after spoonful, focusing entirely on that spot as if nothing else in the world mattered.

It was just after noon when I walked from the restaurant. I was so hell bent on digging I didn't notice how much time had passed, that it went from day to night or even that the spoon had broken, and my hands bled from using what was left of it.

I didn't notice until I heard the double 'whoop' of the police siren and saw the flashlight.

I looked up to the flashlight. Suddenly I was lower, I was in the ground and had dug a hole.

"Harper," it was Officer Lenzi. "What are you doing?"

I didn't answer. I kept moving the dirt.

"Harper, people are worried. They were looking for you. I have been looking for you for a long time. Harper, stop. What are you doing?"

"Digging."

"I see that. What are you digging for?"

"They're here."

"Who is there?" Lenzi asked.

"Cherrie and the others. Two others. Two other little girls."

"Harper, get out of the hole."

"They said they're here. Their ghosts. They led me here." I kept digging. "I have to find them."

"Harper—"

Thud.

I stopped immediately when the sound and feel of that spoon hit upon a solid surface beneath the soil

I looked up.

Lenzi knew it. I knew it.

I found something.

TWENTY-THREE

YET ANOTHER

"What made you come here?" a woman from the news shouted at me as I stood on the other side of the police line.

"Did you have a psychic vision?" another asked. "Are you psychic?"

"Aren't you the ghost lady from online?"

"Did your uncle tell you where the bodies were buried?"

"What?" I asked confused.

Officer Lenzi interceded. "Okay back up from her, she can't tell you anything." He led me away from the media mob. "Go home, Harper," Lenzi told me. "We'll take it from here. I swear I'll call you or stop by tonight to give you an update. You did good." He placed his hand on my arm with a firm squeeze. "Seemed a bit crazy, but you pulled through."

"Maybe now we can find your friend's daughter."

"Anna. Her name is Anna. Hopefully not like this, right?" he looked over his shoulder. "Not like this. Thank you again."

I nodded and thanked him. He was right, I was out of place. The area was taped off, a digging crew came in, along with the coroner and the news.

It was late, I didn't even have a clue where I was or how far I had walked. I asked another officer for directions, and he said it was over a mile to where I had parked my car.

116

Because I was the one who discovered the bodies, or so I believed they were bodies, he offered me a ride.

I declined. It was a nice night, and I wasn't afraid of walking.

Pulling out my phone to check in with Keith, I noticed I had six missed calls from him and one from work.

I dreaded listening to the voicemail from work.

With good reason, too.

"Hi Harper, this is Sergio. In light of the events today, we will no longer be needing your services at Luciano's. Feel free to give me a call if you want to."

Yeah, that wasn't happening. After ending the voicemail, I called Keith.

"Harp!" he blasted. "Where are you? Me and Gal were super worried, then we saw the news story about how a crazy waitress was digging and found bodies."

"Crazy *ex*-waitress."

"You got fired?"

"I did."

"Man."

"It's okay. After all this dies down, I'll get something, until then you will share that monetized site."

"Deal," he said. "What happened?"

"I was serving food, I looked out the window and there was that little girl. Only she wasn't alone. Two more were with her. I followed them."

"You walked out on your job?"

"I wasn't even thinking, Keith. I just went and we walked awhile. I was in this daze or trance. We get to a spot, they say dig,

I dig and the next thing I know, I'm in a hole, it's dark and Lenzi is asking what I'm doing."

"Are you okay?" he asked.

"Not really."

"Why don't you come over."

"You know what? I will. Where's Galen?"

"He's watching Golden Girl reruns with my mom."

"As soon as I walk back to my car, I'll head over. Again, thanks."

I ended my call with Keith and before I put it away, I decided to use the GPS to figure out where I was and how far I had to go. When I saw I still had a good haul, it was disheartening.

Walking to the hidden and buried bodies seemed to take a lot shorter time than walking back.

The bodies.

I stayed at the site for a half hour before Lenzi told me to go.

During my remainder of my walk back to the car, I looked at my phone and to the local stations.

They were fast, already reporting and speculating.

The one local news station was doing a special broadcast and I placed in my earphones to listen.

"Speaking on anonymity," the male reporter said. "They believe there are three bodies. They have pulled the container. The sticker on it is from a store chain that closed. Maybe thirty years ago, but they do believe that's the time frame the victims died. They say the bodies are in remarkable condition. And they are that of three children."

"Heartbreaking," the anchor woman replied. "Is there speculation to who they might be?"

"Well, Lisa, I did some digging. A few of us reporters did. Now, this isn't confirmed, this is our speculation. But there were three girls reported missing around the time of the Mya Stevens case. My research shows Child Killer Earl Easton was prime suspect in the disappearances. But Easton was killed before they could get the information. These three little girls went missing before Mya."

"If I am not mistaken, Mya was killed and found not far from there."

"That's right, Lisa," the male reporter said. "Not far at all. Over to my left you can see the old Aurora Baptist Church, which is where Mya was discovered. Behind there. The three girls missing at the same time were Cherrie Tyrell, eight years old, she went missing on her way home from school. Ten-year-old Connie Doyle, and missing from a bus stop, and four-year-old Samantha Lang, who disappeared from her front yard. All three were from South Buffalo. They say ..."

I paused the news report when I noticed I had made it back to my car. It was a few minutes shy of ten pm and the restaurant was still open. As I approached the corner, I could still see people inside. Wanting to avoid being seen, I detoured another block.

The last thing I wanted was for Sergio to spot me.

As I made it to my car, I saw the flashing blue and red lights. They lit up the area and I knew they came from behind.

The squad car pulled close and that was when I saw it was Officer Lenzi.

"Please don't tell me I lost time again," I said.

"No, I was looking for you," he said. "Get in. I'll drive you to your car."

119

"It's just around the block."

"I know."

I opened the passenger door of the police car and got inside.

"Are you headed home?" Officer Lenzi asked.

"I was going to go to Keith's."

"That's good. There's a lot of press at your apartment building."

"Swell."

"There were three bodies, Harper."

I looked at him.

He continued. "All stuffed inside one of those Rubbermaid bins. Big one, then buried. They weren't killed there. They were killed elsewhere and buried there."

I sighed out and lowered my head.

"They were sealed pretty good, even though it's been decades, the coroner thinks he can get something from the bodies."

I nodded.

"The one, the littlest one had hair in her fist. They think she pulled it from the attacker."

"I told you she was showing me her hand."

Lenzi nodded. "They're gonna try to match DNA so I am giving you the head's up."

"To my uncle?" I asked.

Lenzi nodded.

"So, he was suspected of killing them as well?"

"He was. I told you we suspected him of missing girls."

"But how do we know? The victim that they know for sure he killed, where was she buried."

"She wasn't," Lenzi explained. "He was caught with the girl's body by the Henderson brothers, and he took off. One of the brothers is still alive, if you want to talk …"

"No. Why would I do that?"

"I just wanted you to be prepared. It just seems to me that you don't believe your uncle did it and, well, if you heard someone tell you what they saw—"

"No, it's fine." I saw that we were at the parking lot and my car. "It's just hard. It'll be hard on my mother."

"I know it will. But the family of those three girls will finally have some closure. They owe you for that."

"Thanks." I reached for the handle. "Will you keep me posted?"

"I will. Get some rest."

"I will. Good night." I reached for the door handle and stopped. "Shit."

"What's wrong?"

"My purse is in my locker at the restaurant. They called and fired me. Now I have to go back."

"Wait here. I'll get it."

"Are you sure?"

"I'll be right back." Lenzi pulled over a little, put the car in gear and stepped out.

I waited in the squad car until I saw him returning with my purse, then I got out and met him.

"Um, yeah." He handed me my purse. "They really aren't happy with you. I told them you helped find those missing girls and your boss said that you need to find bodies on your own time."

"Oh my God, that dick."

Lenzi chuckled. "Are you alright to drive?"

"Yep. Thank you." I fished out my keys. "Thanks again." I walked to my car and opened the door. Lenzi lifted his hand in a wave as he drove off and I got inside.

Strapping myself in, keys in the ignition, my eyes cast upward to the rearview mirror.

Anna was in the rectangular reflection.

The missing daughter of Lenzi's friend. My heart skipped a beat and I hurriedly looked behind me. She wasn't in the back seat.

I exhaled, thinking it was just my exhaustion, I turned back around. As soon as I peered in the mirror again she was there.

"Find me," she said,

"Sure." I started my car. "Why not."

TWENTY-FOUR

GETTING WARMER

It wasn't happening again, and I wasn't going alone to be deemed some crazy woman. I explained to Anna through the mirror that I was getting Keith.

It was still a shock to me seeing her there because I would have sworn she wasn't dead. Everyone else from that quad party made an appearance but her.

It was sad and I felt bad for her mother.

I would find her like she asked.

Inside the entrance area by his front door, I spoke in a whispering voice to him. "Get your shoes on. Hurry."

"Why am I helping you find a body?" he asked in a matching whisper.

"I'm not doing it alone."

"It's after ten."

"Oh, like it matters."

Galen inched to us. "Why are we whispering?"

"I don't want to wake Keith's mom."

"She has me …" Keith grunted as he slipped on his shoe. "Going to look for another body."

"More?" Galen asked.

I nodded. "Anna, a young woman came to me."

"I would like to go," said Galen.

Keith stomped his foot into his shoe. "Dude, you have been trying to leave the house all day."

"I don't think it's fair that some spirits can roam freely about." Galen waved his hand around. "And I must stay in this castle. Surely, I cannot protect you. I am here to do so."

I shook my head. "You're here because a car horn beeped."

Keith snapped his finger. "Let me get my wallet in case we get arrested."

"Hurry."

"Oh, please," he turned and looked at me. "Like the body is going anywhere."

"You're so rude. I'll meet you outside." I grabbed the handle of the screen porch door. "I'll be back later, Galen." I pushed it open and took a step, as I did, so did Galen. When I emerged on to the porch, he was there at the same time.

His eyes widened and so did his smile. "I'm out. I'm free!" he shouted. "I am free." He tossed his hands in the air and did a victory jump before, stepping off the porch.

I was stunned.

Keith stepped out. "Whoa. Galen is out. How did that happen?"

I shrugged. "He stepped out when I did."

"Do you think he's connected to you or maybe all we had to do was just open the door for him?"

"Who knows. Let's just go. Get in the car." I hurried over. "Can he sit in a car?"

Keith shrugged. "He should. He sits on the sofa."

I looked at Galen. "You can sit on the sofa?"

Galen nodded. "Yes. Very softly and carefully so I don't sink through."

"Well do the same now. We don't want you sinking through and falling out." I opened the back door. "And don't merge with Anna."

"Left," Anna said. "Here."

I jerked the wheel causing a squealing sound.

"I truly wish I could feel how this carriage moves," Galen commented. "It seems enjoyable. Rose has a reputation of driving hastily like that."

"Who is Rose?" I questioned.

"From the Golden Women Picture show."

"Golden Girls," I corrected, then on Anna's command turned again.

"Why did you turn like that?" Keith asked.

"Anna said turn."

"Where is Anna?"

"If I look in the mirror it looks like she's in the back seat," I explained. "But when I physically look back, she isn't there."

Keith leaned over. "I don't see her in the mirror or the back."

"I do not see her either," added Galen. "One would think one from the other realm could see a spirit from the other realm."

"One would think," I replied, then I spotted the lone streetlight on the dark side road. There were business there, older ones spread out, but under that lone light, the parking lot was not only lit up, but so was the faded sign. 'Henderson Brothers Tires.'

It was the second time in an hour that the name Henderson Brothers was before me.

"Strange," I said softly.

"Yes, it is," Keith replied. "I can't figure out why Galen can't see her either."

"Not that. The tire shop. The brothers that were witness to my Uncle Earl's crime were Henderson Brothers."

"Dude, the tire brothers were the ones that lynched your uncle?"

"They were?" I questioned.

"You didn't know?" Keith stated. "They were part of six men."

"Shit."

"Who are the tire brothers?" Galen asked.

Before I could answer, Anna spoke.

"Please hurry," she said.

"I'm trying," I replied.

"Trying to what?" asked Keith.

"I'm talking to Anna. She wants me to hurry."

"Maybe she can't run fast enough from the light," said Galen. "I ran today with ease. Perhaps the reason I cannot see her is because she is not dead."

I don't know why I did it, but without thinking, my foot just went to the brake.

"What?" Keith asked. "What is it now?"

"What if he's right and she's calling for help?" I glanced into the mirror.

"Ahead," Anna said. "The house. Green awning."

"Are you dead?" I asked her.

"Don't let me be."

I slammed my foot to the gas. "Look for a house with a green awning."

"Is that where she is?" Keith asked.

"Yes, and get ready to call the police. She's not dead."

"What is an awning?" asked Galen. "Green? Would that be it?"

I looked to my left. There was a small house on the corner with a green awning on the tiny front porch. One of those story and a half older homes.

The house was dark, no porch light was on and it looked as if it had been vacant for a while. The grass was high, and the weeds were like bushes.

A faded for sale sign was out front, graffiti was on the tattered siding and two of the windows were boarded,

I hurriedly pulled over. Keith jumped out first as I reached for the glove box to get the little flashlight. Galen followed behind him, leaving the car without ever opening the door.

I looked to the mirror ... no Anna.

My heart sunk.

Oh God what if I waited too long?

Hands trembling, I turned on the flashlight and raced toward the house.

Keith was trying to open the front door. I didn't see Galen.

"Maybe this isn't it," Keith said. "It's dark."

"She said this is it."

"Want me to break a window?"

"We need to get inside. She wasn't in the mirror, Keith."

"Harper, I don't know what to tell you. Let's call Lenzi and tell him—"

"Keith! Harper!" Galen's voice sounded echoey. "In the rear of the structure."

127

Both Keith and I raced from the porch. There was so much junk buried it the weeds, it was like an obstacle course.

As soon as we got to Galen, he passed through the wall of the home and went inside.

The back windows were completely boarded, but through a space in the boards, I could see a speck of light.

I tried to peek in.

"She is here," Galen said, "Call your authorities. I think she needs a medicine man."

"Call 911," I told Keith and pulled at the boards. It was useless. I wasn't strong enough. How did she get in there?

"What is the address?"

"I don't know. Go around front," I said rushed, then ran to the back door. The storm door, woodened and weather worn, was off the hinges and the back door was ajar. Clearly it had been jammed open.

I raced inside and followed the light.

I entered through a kitchen, tiles were lifted, and the ceiling was falling down in spots. The light came from what would have been the dining room. A singled battery-operated lantern was on a box. There were empty cans of food scattered about, a duffle bag with clothes half out of it.

In the center of the room was a mattress, and on it was Anna.

Galen stood above her. "I do not think she was alone here. Perhaps her friend went for help?"

I raced to Anna and when I saw the needle still in her arm, I knew that wasn't the case. If there was someone with her, they didn't go for help, they just ran.

Dropping to the floor, I placed my hands on her. "She's still warm. She's still warm."

"If her body is still warm, the soul still remains," Galen said.

"You're right. You're right." I didn't know if it was the right thing to do or not, but I removed the needle, and pulled Anna from the mattress to the solid hard floor.

I felt for a pulse but didn't find one, nor did I hear any breath sounds.

Even though she was warm, her lips were blue, I could see that in the dim light.

I had to try. I had to try to do something.

Keith rushed in. "Help is on the way. Oh my God. Is she?"

"I don't know," I replied, then dove into doing CPR.

<><><><>

The red lights of the ambulances flashed steadily, lighting up the empty house.

I watched the paramedics take Anna on a stretcher. My attempts were futile, but they were able to revive her. For how long and what would happen next, remained to be seen.

While the police surrounded the area, I had Keith hide Galen.

His presence would be hard to explain.

I couldn't believe what had happened or the day that I had.

A police officer approached me. "Officer Lenzi said he'll talk to you tomorrow at the station to get your statement. Are you alright?"

I nodded. "Yes, thank you."

"Good job," he told me then walked away.

I looked around the house, it was so sad. I would never understand what happened with Anna and why.

Wanting nothing more than to just go back to Keith's and eat some of his mother's leftovers, I walked out of the house and headed to my car.

Officer Lenzi stepped out of his squad car.

"Hey," he said, walking up to me. "Aren't you the busy lady tonight?"

"It's crazy."

"My God, Harper, this is unreal."

"Do we know how she is?"

"We won't know. We're looking for the boyfriend now," he said. "We think he was here and left."

I nodded.

"You need some rest," he said.

"And food, yeah. I'm going to Keith's."

"If I hear anything about the bodies or Anna, I'll let you know. Harper, how did you find her?"

"She came to me," I replied. "She came. I can't explain it and I don't know how it happened."

"Well, whatever happened, four mothers are sleeping easier tonight because of you. Four mothers now know what happened to their children. You did excellent. Who knows? Maybe with this gift, you can help a lot more people."

"I thought so, too."

"What do you mean 'thought'?" he asked.

"Ryan, I can't do this anymore. I have to make it stop.

"Why?"

"I don't know. Just a feeling. All this good and I just know it won't be long before something really bad comes through," I crossed my arms to shiver off the chill. "And we're not going to be able to stop it."

TWENTY-FIVE

CHAT WITH BABA

Keith was such a regular and frequent visitor at Baba's assisted living center, that he had no problem picking her up for the day. I got the third degree, had to show forms and do a background check.

It was insulting. Especially since Keith wasn't even blood related. Then my friend told me it wasn't the first time he took her out. He didn't want to get in trouble with me, but he took Baba to the casino and track once a month.

I just really wanted to spend time with Baba outside of her home

Plus, I wanted her to meet Galen.

She spent the day with us at Keith's house. Millie made veal breast with tiny potatoes and creamed peas.

I spoke to her about all that had happened and where I was mentally with it.

Her frail fingers wrapped around my hand as she sat at the dining table enjoying her wine and meal.

"You have done well, Little One," she said. "The choice is yours. That is all I ever wanted."

"I feel that I am abandoning a gift," I said.

"How?" asked Baba. "You have used the gift to help many. If you feel the need to let it go, then you let it go."

"A couple things have to happen first."

"Like?"

"I just need some sort of confirmation about Uncle Earl."

Baba shook her head. "I never understood that. I knew Earl. Such a sweet boy."

"What was the story, Baba?" I asked. "I mean was he arrested? Out on bail when he was beaten to death?"

"No. They say witnesses saw a man with the body of the girl and he took off. Your Uncle was at work at the print shop working late when the men came for him. One of the men had witnessed him. And they chased him and beat him, then tossed him in the river."

"That doesn't make sense," I said. "I mean. If the men saw him, why didn't they turn him in?"

"Cowboy justice."

I sat back. "Was one of the men a Henderson brother?"

"I don't remember. But if you need to know the truth, put it in your mind." She pointed to her own temple. "Think it. The answers will come. The truth will emerge."

"Thank you."

"What are the other reasons?" Baba asked.

"Excuse me?"

"You said a couple things have to happen first before you let go of the gift."

"Yeah, I'm doing this sleep study tonight. It will monitor me. I'm curious to see what physical things happen with my body when I go into the state."

"That's interesting. Will you share the results?"

"I will." I nodded. "And the other thing." I pointed to Galen who stood in the corner of the room. "Him. He has to go back to the light."

Galen stepped forward. "I cannot go back. There is a reason I am here."

"Yeah," I said. "Because you were touching me when I woke up."

"Fate has me here. There is something I must do. If there were not something of importance, I would not still be here."

"That's not fate," I said. "That's you running from the light."

Baba chuckled. "He will return when he feels it is right."

"Thank you, Elder." Galen bowed. "I pray that all people around you welcome and absorb the wisdom of your years. It is a great honor to be in the presence of one who has lived on the earth for so long."

"Isn't he sweet." Baba smiled.

"Oh, he's a pip," I said sarcastically. "But he's not that bad."

"I wish I could go to the slumber study she plans to attend tonight," said Galen. "I cannot protect her if I am not there."

"No worries," I told him. 'It's a controlled environment. Lots of people there. I'll be fine."

"Are you sure?" Baba asked. "Maybe you should bring him."

"How do I explain his presence?"

"Obviously these people know why you're there."

"No." I shook my head. "I'll be fine."

Baba gazed up at Galen. "I like knowing he will protect you. He can do so on a different level."

"And know this," Galen said. "I will. But when fate takes her soul, I gave my word, in the afterlife, I will take her as my wife.

She deserves a husband since she has not found one in her advancing years. My repayment for this gift of coming back."

'That's so sweet of you," Baba said. "That makes me happy to know she won't be alone in the afterlife."

"I appreciate the marriage thing," I told him. "God willing, it will be a while."

"I'll wait."

"On the other side, right?" I asked.

Galen nodded. "Yes. After I know I have done what I am here to do. And," he just stopped.

"And?" I asked.

"And how do you say it, oh Millie told me ..." He paused to think. "Yes. When I finish binge watching the entire series of Golden Girls."

TWENTY-SIX

GO TO SLEEP

Dashing.

There was no other word to describe the sleep study technician.

With his short wavy hair, sculpted face and perfect teeth, Jon, the tech was more camera ready than Donner Greg, the host of the television show I-Team. An investigative show that was paying for everything.

Donner Greg wasn't bad looking for a middle-aged man. He probably would have looked better without all that pancake makeup that seemed to show every crease in his face.

There was nothing more unnerving than knowing I was going to be in an uncontrolled sleep state with someone as handsome as Jon standing at a monitor twenty feet from me.

It wasn't a normal sleep study lab. It was one adjusted for me. Cameras that would monitor everything.

They prepped me in another room entirely. I wore a modified version of a hospital gown with a long pajama like bottoms. My hand ached a little from the intravenous line they had placed in me. It wasn't connected to anything yet.

The best technicians and the top sleep study doctor in the country were there. Along with Donner Greg, of course.

"You know how this will work," Donner walked me to the sleep study room. "We have cameras and thermal imaging. We're gonna try to capture anything we can."

"We can't be sure anything will happen," I replied.

"Maybe you can try." He winked.

When he said that, immediately I heard Baba's voice, *'If you need to know the truth, put it in your mind. The truth will emerge.'*

"I'll try," I replied.

"Good. We'll do the post interview tomorrow sometime. I have an intro to film, then I'll leave you to it. Right now, this." He opened the door.

The room reminded me of the surgical theaters I would see on television or movies. A large room with windows near the ceiling. Windows that led to an observation room.

A nice comfy bed was set up in the middle of the room. Monitors were near it and across the room was where Jon would stand.

He introduced me to the two men and woman in the room. One was Jon, whom I met earlier, then Denise, a nurse and the doctor.

The somnologist, Doctor Johan Strauss, was a man in his late fifties. His hair was a little wild and wiry. He presented himself as a gentle soul. He would be in the office behind Jon watching everything as well.

"Above all," Johan said. "Jon and I are monitoring the medical aspects of this all. You mentioned that you are worried you stop breathing?"

I nodded. "When I come out of the episodes, I gasp. It's like I don't have any air."

He made a notation in his chart. "We will watch for that and let you know."

"That's only when I lucid dream," I explained. "If I don't lucid dream, I think everything is normal."

"Is when you lucid dream when you claim to go to the other side?" he asked.

"It's when I *do* go to the other side," I clarified.

"Lucid dreams occur during REM and your subconscious switches on," he explained. "The mild sedative we give you will keep your body rested even if your mind snaps to consciousness."

"Wait. Wait." Donner held up his hand. "So even if she's lucid, she won't be able to wake up."

"It'll be hard."

"We want her to wake up, to pull something through." Donner said.

"And if her heart stops beating in such an event," Johan explained. "Then it's occurring when her body suddenly goes from deep sleep to awake. That's dangerous."

"No, maybe because she's on the other side?" Donner asked. "Maybe she needs to have her heart not beating to do this."

"If that's the case, she can't keep doing it," Johan explained. "We'll find out. If her heart stops. We'll get it beating again."

"But she won't pull anything through if she doesn't wake up to do it," Donner said.

"Mr. Greg," Johan was firm. "This is not a circus. You wanted to see what happened medically with her while in a state where she claims to go to the other side. I will be able to show you that. If you want a side show where she pulls something through, this is not the place. I want this woman safe. I can allow her to sleep and get to the place. But she will be there briefly and retreat to normal REM. But we will be able to see physically what is happening."

Donner huffed. "Fine."

"I can do it without sleeping," I told him. "If you want something for the show, I can do it. Galen would have to be there."

"The Spartan soldier?" Donner asked.

I nodded.

"Awesome. Okay, deal." Donner stood. "Let's do the sleep study thing. It will be a nice scientific angle to add."

"And with that." Johan stood. "Mr. Greg and I will leave you to it. Good luck, Ms. Monroe."

"Thank you."

"I'll be watching from up there." Donner pointed to the high windows.

Swell, I thought, *no pressure.*

After Johan and Donner left, I sat on the bed and Jon and Denise walked over.

"Normally," Denise said. "There's no sedatives in sleep studies. Lay back and relax. I need to run the line."

I knew what she meant. She had to place the tubing from the intravenous bagging into the catheter that had already been introduced into my vein.

I laid down, placing the covers over me while Denise worked with the tubing.

Jon approached. "We need to hook you up to monitors for your heart, breathing and brain activity."

"And I'll actually be able to sleep?" I asked. "I doubt that."

"No, you will." Dashing Jon smiled. "Within minutes you'll be out. No worries though. Me and Denise will be right here in this room."

"Let's get the monitors all hooked up to you." Denise showed me the wires. "Then you just think pleasant thoughts."

Pleasant thoughts.

Again, my mind when directly to what Baba had said.

'If you need to know the truth, put it in your mind. The truth will emerge.'

I would, along with thoughts of Uncle Earl.

TWENTY-SEVEN

UNCLE EARL AGAIN

It didn't take long for the medicinal cocktail to kick in. I felt relaxed and then tired. Both Jon and Denise were near me and both looked at me as if they knew I was about to fall asleep.

Once I shut my heavy eyes, that was it.

I wasn't sure when it transitioned from dreamless sleeping. I was certain I had been dreaming, but didn't register it until I found myself standing a block away from the old church. The one closed down and condemned. The same church that was near where I found the bodies of the three girls.

Only it wasn't overgrown and it wasn't dark. In fact, it was bright and sunny. Cars moved down the street and they were much older cars.

It was as if I had been transported back in time.

Then I recalled what my thoughts were, my intentions set before I fell asleep.

Was it happening?

I knew I was dreaming; it was lucid. I thought it wasn't supposed to happen.

But it did.

I was there. Unlike other dreams, no one seemed to see me. I realized that when *they* passed right through me.

A man and a little girl. He held her hand and they walked.

She peered up to him so innocently. He didn't look back. I only saw him from behind, but I knew who it was.

Uncle Earl.

And the child, I knew her face. I had seen it in the newspaper articles. It was the child no one in my family ever mentioned by name. It was always the little girl.

Her name was Amanda. She deserved to be known by her name.

They walked ahead of me, down the street, then flash.

Like a huge bulb went off in my face, everything faded to white then back again. Only this time, I was standing twenty feet from them in the playground.

I couldn't see Amanda fully, Uncle Earl was pushing her on the swing.

Just as I stepped closer …

Flash.

I watched them walk into the church.

My heart started to beat faster, I could feel it. I moved quickly toward the church. When my foot took the first step on those stairs, everything whitewashed again.

Then came the scream.

A child's scream. A horrendous painful cry that was like a knife to my chest. The cry was so fearful, that poor baby had to be so scared. I could feel it. I could feel her terror.

Flash.

I gasped.

I was in the woods. I saw Amanda's wide eyes, her face drawn of life. Uncle Earl knelt above her, pulling back his hands from her throat.

"Oh my God," I said aloud, immediately, I began to cry.

Slowly his head turned. Did he hear me? No. It was to the sound of running footsteps.

"Dear God," a man's voice said from behind me. "What did you do? Not again. Not again."

As I went to look at who it was, Uncle Earl turned his head.

Only it wasn't Uncle Earl.

The hair was the same, the build, but the face was not.

"Wes, come on," the man behind me said. "We can't keep—"

"You." The man with Amanda, Wes, looked right at me and smiled.

It was a sinister smile and he laughed. His left front tooth was chipped.

"I've been waiting for you. Thank you for coming." He slowly stood up.

Everything suddenly grew gray and overcast, the leaves on the trees were gone and everything looked dead.

I backed up as he moved to me.

I needed to get away from him.

Wake up. Wake up. I told myself. But nothing. I wasn't waking.

I spun on my heels to run. The ground was uneven. I was no longer in the woods, I was somewhere else.

Wake up. Wake up.

The earth looked like black tree roots twisted around burnt skulls. Every step I took, I screamed in my mind to wake up. He pursued me calling my name in a chilling, taunting manner.

"Harper. Harper."

What I could only describe as moans of damnation rang out all around me. Arms reached from the ground, grabbing for me.

"Harper, wait for me," he said.

Wake up. Wake up. I pushed and tried to awaken. To get out of wherever I was.

"Help us," the souls cried out.

"Wake up!" I screamed.

Snap.

Gasp.

Beep. Beep. Beep.

I opened my eyes, trying to sit up. I was still connected to the machines.

The room was calm with only a dim light. Jon stood, looking down to a computer on one of those rolling carts.

I shifted my eyes, breathing heavily. Was it real? Was I awake? There were no spirits in the room. None that I could see lurking.

Denise smiled as she stood from behind the desk. "You okay, Harper?"

I nodded. "Yeah. Was everything alright?"

"I'll check the monitors." She walked over toward Jon. "I think a little jump there at the end, but everything looks normal."

I exhaled in relief. "No one came through?"

She smiled in a quirky 'don't be silly' way and shook her head.

Then Jon calmly said, "Yes."

"What?" Denise asked him.

"Someone came through."

"Jon, don't tease," Denise scolded. "That's not—"

She never got her last word out. In lightning speed, almost too fast for me to register or react, Jon pushed aside the computer cart. He put both his hands on the sides of her face, lifted her up slightly then with a hard, quick turn, and snap, he broke her neck.

I screamed just as her body dropped to the floor, trying to get up, but was tangled in the wires and tubing.

At that point I didn't care if the needles ripped my skin, I yanked at them as I jumped from the bed, going to the other side of it as Jon raged to me.

As if it weighed nothing, he shoved the bed out of the way, lunged to me and grabbed my throat.

"Jon!" Johan yelled out. "Stop right there!"

Behind Jon I saw my sleep doctor. He held a revolver.

"Let her go," Johan ordered. "I hit the button for security. Let her go."

Then he did. With ease, hand still on my throat, he tossed me aside.

I banged into the end of the discarded bed, smacking my hip before falling to the floor.

I thought for sure he was going after Johan, but I guess by the sound of it, he ran out.

On the floor, I couldn't really see beyond the bed. It was hard to breathe, my throat felt crushed.

Johan raced over and down to me. "We'll get you help. Don't move. I don't know what came over Jon. I've known him for years."

"That wasn't," I swallowed. It was hard to talk. "That wasn't Jon."

"What do you mean?"

145

Immediately, everything hit me. Every emotion I could imagine, fear, sadness, grief. "Oh, God," I wept. "What did I do? What did I pull through?"

TWENTY-EIGHT

THE AFTER

Doctor Johan Strauss wasn't a big drinker, but he kept a bottle of cucumber vodka in his bottom desk drawer for the occasional sip.

I was grateful for that and I downed two dixie cups like it was water. So fast I didn't taste the cucumber.

"Now let's get you to the ER wing," Johan said.

"No, I'm fine."

"You're not fine. Your side is bruised, you took a tumble. Let me get you checked out."

"You're a doctor."

He nodded. "I am, but I'm not superman. I don't have Xray vision. I don't know if that hip is broken or not."

"It's not broken. I'm standing on it."

"Your voice still sounds funny. We need to check that Larynx."

"I'm fine," I repeated.

The hip was painful, but it didn't feel broken. I could move it, and my throat didn't really hurt too much. Just an ache. It all paled in comparison to the pain I felt over what had all happened.

Security arrived shortly after I had been thrown to the floor. The room was swarming with police. One county detective told us not to leave, but I could go upstairs to get treatment.

I didn't want to.

I just wanted to go home. Or rather to Keith's. I felt safe going there. Even though Galen wasn't of flesh and blood, I believed because of what he was, a ghost, he was a sense of protection like he had said.

When I called Keith, I told him not to tell my mother. And I asked him to try to get a hold of Mag, her number was on his fridge.

He said he'd try.

I told him I'd be there as fast as I could.

Denise's body was still on the floor. It was covered with a tarp. Officers and the medical examiner took pictures.

That poor woman. I hoped she didn't have children that wondered why their mother didn't come home.

It broke my heart to think about it.

"Do you think she suffered?" I asked Johan.

Johan shook his head. "No, I don't. She didn't see it coming."

"Harper!" Lenzi's voice carried to me.

I turned to see him walk in. He was in unform.

"Are you alright?" he asked with rushed concern.

"She needs checked out," said Johan.

"Then get checked out," Lenzi said.

"I'm fine."

"She's not fine," argued Johan. "I think that hip is broken. And look at her neck."

"My hip is not broken. I just want to go home. Or rather Keith's."

Lenzi nodded. "That's a good call. They'll put a squad car on the house. I had no idea it was you until the chief told me." He exhaled. "He's killed three people on his way out of here."

My eyes widened. "I didn't know."

Johan shook his head. "I didn't either."

"This guy is dangerous," said Lenzi. "He's really dangerous."

"That's an understatement," I replied. "He's—"

With excitement that didn't match the feel of the room, Donner Greg called my name. "Harper Monroe, you are unbelievable." He stepped in farther. "I'm with her. Excuse me. Sorry." He paused at Denise's body. "Whoa." He carried a tablet in his hand and rushed over. "You are unbelievable. I just reviewed the footage. This is television like never before." He held the tablet my way.

"You have footage?" Lenzi asked. "You can't have footage that's evidence."

"It's my footage. My cameras."

"You can't show that to people. Again, it's evidence."

"Yes, officer, I am well aware," Donner said. "And I'll get the appropriate court orders to be able to show it. But right now, Harper, you have to look at this. First, the regular camera. Watch Jon."

I watched the video play. I was laying still on the bed, not moving. It looked like nothing out of the ordinary. Jon flinched just a tiny bit, it could have been my imagination. Donner stopped the video when Denise walked over to Jon.

"No need to see that again." Donner swiped the tablet. "Now look at the thermal. Same clip."

I had never seen a thermal image. You just see outlines of items that give off heat. Jon, Denise and I were all the same color.

"Now watch."

When he said that, a split second before I sat up, a blue figure shot across the room from out of nowhere and into Jon.

Jon's thermal imaging when from shades of red to blue then back to red.

"Holy shit," Lenzi explained. "Show that again."

"With pleasure." Donner did.

"Oh my God." Lenzi's hand went over his mouth. "What was that?"

I shook my head. "You said Jon was dangerous. Yeah, he is. Because that's not Jon. Whatever that was. Whatever went in him," I whispered. "Is not human."

TWENTY-NINE

TWISTED VISION

Mag is on her way back, the text message from Keith read, *she will be in tomorrow afternoon.*

Seeing that text made me feel better and relieved.

I sighed out pretty heavily upon reading it.

"We really prefer you to stay," the emergency room doctor handed me my discharge papers.

"Do I stand a chance of dying if I don't?"

"No."

"I want to leave."

"I get that. But once the orthopedic specialist looks at your films, we may need you to come back."

"If that's the case, I will."

"If the pain gets too bad come back."

I nodded. "Thank you." Then noticed Lenzi with a wheel-chair.

"Are you ready?" he asked, putting on the brakes to the chair.

"Officer," the ER doctor called him. "Talk some sense into her."

"That's not gonna happen," Lenzi replied. "I don't think it's about staying here, as much as it is going home to get something she needs."

"Can you go get it?" he asked.

Lenzi shook his head. "Unfortunately, she is the only one who can."

I sat in the chair, careful not to show how much it hurt.

"Good luck, Miss Monroe."

I thanked the doctor as Lenzi backed me out.

"So what I do I need from home that only I can get?" I asked.

"Galen, of course."

"Of course."

"Plus, Mag is showing up. We need to know what she says."

He wheeled me from the emergency room to the squad car waiting outside. Lenzi said they'd come back for my car, he just didn't want me driving.

After helping me in and getting me situated, we headed to Keith's.

"Can I ask you something?" I said. "I know it's a beaten horse with you."

"What?" Lenzi chuckled the words. "What conversation is a beaten horse?"

"The Henderson Brothers."

"Ah." He nodded. "Not a beaten horse. What about them?"

"Did you ever find it suspicious that they just happened upon my uncle and the girl's body, never called the cops, just waited until that night and killed him."

"First, let's get the chain of events right."

"You told me that."

"No, I told you they saw him with the body and he took off. That was cliff notes. They weren't sure who he was. They had to find out. They didn't know at first the child was dead until he took off."

"Did they call the police?"

"To report the death, yeah. What's going on?"

"My Uncle Earl didn't kill her," I said. "He's not a killer."

"Harper, stop, you of all people know he is."

"No. I of all people know he's not. The hair in the hand of the girl. When that comes up not a DNA match to Earl, that will prove it."

"That he didn't kill that girl," Lenzi said. "I'm sure it's gonna come back a match. Why are you so sure he's innocent?"

"Because I think one of the Henderson brothers killed those four girls. When I was in the sleep study, I went to the other side. I was there. I saw Amanda—"

"Wait. Stop. Who is Amanda?" Lenzi asked.

"The little girl they say my Uncle was seen with, the one found behind the church."

Lenzi shook his head. "That was Mya Stevens. There was no Amanda."

"I swore her name was Amanda. I saw a man strangling her. His hands on her throat. I was like the ghost. The man doing the strangling was not my Uncle Earl. Another man came from behind me and was upset. Said something about not again. Called him Wes."

"Wes Henderson. He's the brother that died. Took his own life not long after the Earl thing."

"So they confessed to the lynching?" I asked.

"No, it was assumed, but there was never any proof. Maybe there's another girl," Lenzi spoke almost in a daze as if he were in thought. "Maybe it's not connected."

"It has to be."

"Might not be. I mean that girl and being caught could be the reason Wes took his own life, not Earl."

"Wes killed those other girls."

"Maybe but … the other girls were killed differently."

"How?" I asked. "You said they were strangled."

"Not with bare hands. With a shoestring."

I sat back and sighed. "What did I see?"

"What time is it?"

"Huh?"

Lenzi picked up his phone. "Okay it's still open."

"What is?"

"A place we may get answers." He quickly turned the wheel.

We drove for only a half block when he pulled the car over directly in front of Marlin's Bar and Grill.

"You want to get a drink, right now?" I asked then I saw it. The Henderson Brothers truck.

Lenzi got out and opened my door. "If someone knows the truth about that day it's Jeremy Henderson. It's been about thirty years, if he's gonna tell the truth he's going to do it now."

"How did you know he would be here?"

Lenzi huffed out a chuckle as he opened the bar door for me. "He's been coming here every night since he turned twenty-one. Anyone that's looking for him know this is where you'll find him."

We walked in. There were only a few people that I could see. The long bar was to the right, a few tables in the center and all down the left side were booths that extended straight to the back room.

Lenzi looked around.

"Officer Lenzi, what can I do for you?" the bartender asked.

"Hey, Geo. I saw his truck out there," Lenzi replied. "I don't see Henderson. Doesn't he usually sit at the bar."

"Usually. A friend came to see him tonight, they went in the back. Just took them a round a few minutes ago."

"Is the friend still here?"

"Probably."

Lenzi have an up nod of his chin. "Thank you." He looked at me. "Can you walk or should I get him."

"Do you mind if I just sit. It's really hard to walk."

"Sure." He waved to Geo. "Giver her what she wants." He placed money on the bar. "Sit," he said to me. "I'll be right back."

"What will it be?" Geo asked,

"Whiskey and soda on the rocks."

The bar stool was easy to sit on. It hurt me some, but I didn't have to climb and lower myself. It was the perfect height.

The bartender poured me a drink as Lenzi went to the back.

I thanked him, told him to keep the change, and brought the tiny straw to my lips.

The first drink entered my mouth when I saw Lenzi. He returned to the room with a commanding rush. He held his radio and was lowering it from his mouth.

"Geo," Lenzi called out, speaking hurriedly. "Did you see the friend leave at all?"

"No. I was just back there not even ten minutes ago. I can check the register to see what time I rang it in."

"No." Lenzi shook his head. "No one leaves at all. I need everyone to stay put," he ordered. "More police are on their way."

"Christ," said Geo. "What happened? Is Henderson okay?"

Lenzi didn't answer him, he looked at me.

"Ryan?" I said his name with question.

Lenzi just shook his head.

That gave me all the answers I needed. I lifted my drink and took a big gulp. Lenzi didn't need to say it. I knew by his demeanor and look on his face.

It wasn't good.

Henderson was dead.

THIRTY

DOORS, DOORS, DOORS

"Yep," Geo's finger tapped the screen of my phone. "That's him."

Like at the sleep study, the bar was swarming with police and investigators. They had to call them in from county and Buffalo because Aurora City didn't have enough.

Second crime scene in three hours.

The other three were at the hospital, Possessed Jon's escape kills. But it was obvious he sought out Jeremy.

When Geo was describing the friend, Lenzi had me contact Donner for a screen shot of Jon.

"Pretty boy," Geo said. "Doesn't look like a killer. Are we sure he did this."

"Anyone else in here that you think may have done it?" Lenzi asked.

Geo shook his head. "No, Jeremy was a good man."

"Good men ..." I finished my drink causing the straw to do a slurping sound. "Don't get their throats sliced for no reason. Unless he was robbed."

"I know he wasn't robbed," Geo replied. "I have his wallet. He always makes me hold it so he doesn't spend money on the, well, games."

"Poker machines," Lenzi corrected. "Call them what they are."

"Hey, they're legal."

I slurped the last few drops.

Lenzi cringed. "Can you get her another drink, please. Do you want another, Harper?"

"Yes, thank you."

"You paying for that one, too?" asked Geo.

"I don't have any money," I said. "I'm still wearing the hospital clothes."

"She doesn't have money."

"I put twenty on the bar fifteen minutes ago," Lenzi said. "How much was her drink?"

"Not twenty. She said keep the change."

Lenzi begrudgingly put another twenty on the bar. "And don't keep the change on this one."

"Cheap bastard." Geo stepped away to get my drink.

Lenzi leaned on the bar to talk to me. "So, tell me again … what? Why are you staring at me like that?"

"That was rude."

"What was?"

"Telling him not to keep the change. That's how he makes his living. I should know, that's how I make my living."

"Made," Lenzi corrected. "Last I knew you were fired."

I gasped. "Oh my God. Way to throw my failures in my face."

Geo set down my drink. "You'll get that from cheap people. Here's your …" He slammed down bills. "Change."

After a long sigh Lenzi looked at me. "Anyhow, tell me again, what you saw when you did this sleep study."

"I was by the church, only it wasn't overgrown. The cars were old. I saw him walking with the girl, then pushing the swing. I never saw his face and I thought it was my Uncle Earl. Then when

I saw him after he killed her, and the man called his name, he turned his head. I saw it wasn't my uncle."

Lenzi nodded. "And the other guy used the name Wes?"

"Yes."

"Hey, Geo," Lenzi called him. "You said you had Jeremy's wallet, can I see it?"

"Why? You want to take his money?"

"Oh my God. There's been a murder, can we just be serious for a second. Please, may I see the wallet?"

Geo huffed, went behind the bar, grabbed the old, tattered brown wallet and handed it to Lenzi.

"What are you doing?" I asked.

Lenzi immediately started to rummage through it. "A hunch." He kept looking. "Yes." He pulled something out. "Just as I thought. Guys tend to keep old pictures in their wallet." He placed an old, folded polaroid on the bar. "Him." He pointed to the man on the left.

That man, that face I would never forget.

"That's him. That's who I saw," I said.

"Wes," stated Lenzi.

Geo audibly cringed. "Wes was a bastard. I knew him in school."

"Did he touch you?" Lenzi whispered. "I know that's how it's done."

I shook my head. "No, but I was running. I don't know. Do you think Earl jumped in him?"

"I do."

I was focused on Lenzi when my ringing phone caused me to jump. I looked at the caller ID. "Shit."

159

"Keith?" Lenzi asked

"No, Mag." I hurriedly answered it. "Mag, hello."

"Well, I hear you got yourself in a pickle," Mag said. "Didn't I tell you to stop?"

"I wanted to do a sleep study," I defended.

"I'm on my way back."

"I know. Thank you."

"Where are you?"

"At a bar right now." I sipped my drink.

"Lord, woman, now is not the time to be partying."

"I'm not partying. Trust me this is not a party. He took another life."

"Listen to what I am going to tell you. You need to go somewhere safe right now. Hide. Let Keith know, I'll come to you. We'll figure this out," she said. "Until then, stay safe. You opened a door, and he knows you can close it. He's coming for you."

I barely muttered out my understanding when she hung up. I stared at the phone. "She is so mysterious."

"What did she say?" Lenzi asked.

"She said I needed to hide. To stay safe."

"Police station," Lenzi said.

"No," Geo grumbled. "Take her to the hospital. Heck, it's like Fort Knox at night. I had a harder time getting in there to see my wife than when I went to county jail to see my nephew. Plus, she's dressed for it."

"I want to go to Keith's," I said.

"We will, but to get Galen, then I think Geo's right. We go back to the hospital. We can post a guard on the door."

"See, I give good advice," Geo said. "Despite you not tipping." He walked away.

"So you think Mag is right?" I leaned closer to Lenzi speaking soft. "She said he wants to make sure I don't close that door. She said he's coming for me."

"Oh, yeah, without a doubt she's right, but not for any door. If what you said was real, was the truth, and Jon is now Wes …" Lenzi looked down at the picture of Wes. "He's taking out witnesses."

THIRTY-ONE

BEING HIP

It had been a long time since I was in a hospital. I barely remembered the experience. I knew enough to know it had changed.

The day and night before had been insanity.

First the sleep study, then Denise's murder, then Jeremy at Marlin's. By the time we made it back to the hospital with Galen, and I was given a room, it was pushing three in the morning and I wasn't done.

I had answered so many questions about what I saw. The problem was I just couldn't tell them that it wasn't Jon committing the murders, it was whatever or whoever was in him.

I mean I could have told them, but they'd think I was nuts.

The ER doctor was still on duty and was glad to see me return.

To be honest, my hip was killing me and my throat ached badly.

He put in for a room. Lenzi on behalf of the police intervened and insisted I didn't have a roommate. Then Mag called and claimed financial responsibility and insisted I'd be given the biggest private room they had.

The staff called it the Queen's room because it was rumored that Aretha Franklin had stayed in that room. That was the cool thing, I wondered if Aretha would come see me.

The room was big, one bed and a sofa. It reminded me of the time my friend Chrissy had a baby and it looked like the family suite.

The rule was placed down that it was one medical personnel at a time in my room.

The orthopedic doctor obviously had never been in the room. He whistled when he walked in. "Look at this room." His accent was predominant when he spoke. Not sure it would be called an accent. It was English or Australian. I'd have to hear him speak more. "Hi, I'm Doctor Brewster. I'm your orthopedic surgeon."

"Did they bring you in from overseas just for me?"

"Is that a joke?"

"Um."

"Are you a celebrity?"

I snorted a laugh, "No. And I got it." I snapped my finger. "You're from England."

"I am. But I did not come across the pond for you. My wife brought me here."

"Oh, cool."

"So why the luxury suite?" he asked. "And the guards? Seems a bit much. That's why I asked if you were a celebrity."

"No, I'm a marked woman. Someone wants to kill me."

"Not me." He lifted his hands. "And you'll be happy to know you'll still be safe tomorrow. You're probably in the safest room in the hospital."

"Okay, where's that?"

"Surgery. We're putting in a pin. You broke your hip."

"What!" I blasted. "There's no way."

"Way."

"No, seriously. It only hurts when I move."

He smiled. "That's funny. Actually, it isn't a bad break, but we do need to stabilize it. I have you scheduled for eleven am. Nothing to eat after dinner tonight. Alright?"

I nodded.

"It'll be fine and quick. Any questions, have the nurse call me."

"I will, thank you."

He gave a nod of goodbye and left.

Galen emerged from the bathroom. I had left the bathroom door open so he could hide there and not scare the nurses, doctors or food service workers.

"What is this pin he speaks of?"

"Something they have to do with my hip. It's broke."

"And they can repair that?"

"Yes, they can."

"Amazing. I was worried when I heard him say you broke it that they would spare you of your suffering."

"You mean kill me?" I asked.

"Yes. Very honorable."

"And stupid. We don't do that anymore."

"Medicine has come a long way. I have seen that while watching the Golden Girls."

"Uh yeah," I said, laughing. "It's a different millennium. It's come a long way." I cleared my throat to chase away the laugh. "Hey, Galen, in all seriousness, I am glad to have you watch over me during times that are humanly impossible.'

"I will do what I can."

"Unfortunately," her voice entered the room. "He can do nothing against a human form." Mag walked all the way in. Keith was with her. "How are you?" she questioned.

"I'm good," I replied. "I broke my hip."

"Dude!" Keith commented. "Like my aunt Midge."

"Yep, just like her."

"She still hobbles. She keeps saying, 'someone put me out of my misery'."

"Ha!" Galen charged out. "See, it would still be a useful practice in this day."

Keith looked at me. "What is he talking about?"

I shook my head. "Nothing. Mag, thank you for coming."

"I promised your mother I'd watch out for you." She pulled up a chair and sat down, looking at Galen. "You are our soldier?"

"I am madam." He slightly bowed. "It is an honor."

"And it is an honor to meet you. Are you ready to do your job?"

"I am."

"Good." Mag looked at me again. "Listen, you are very safe in this room."

"I'm supposed to have surgery tomorrow. I'm scared because they'll put me under, and I can't have Galen in the room. It's the strangest thing. He can't walk through doors. And I don't think they'll have the OR door open."

Mag crinkled her nose. "No, they won't. We'll figure out something. We'll have to. Some entities can pass through doors. Some cannot. This was a problem for Lincoln, too."

"Andrew Lincoln the actor?" I asked.

"No, President Lincoln."

"Mag?" Keith spoke up. "He's dead."

"No, shit," she snapped. "What the hell do you think I do? President Obama wanted advice and called me in for Lincoln. But Obama can't stand still. Has a pacing problem. He'd talk to Lincoln, start walking with him like Lincoln was a normal member of his team. He'd go in a room and be talking to himself. Poor Abe was left in the hall. The man could run from the light though."

Galen stood straight. "I can run very well from the light."

"Yeah, until you're in a room with no exit," Mag said. "But then again you know that." She faced me again. "Listen, I believe one hundred percent that he is coming for you. Not to alarm you, but I had that cop friend of yours put guards on your parents, Keith's parents and your Baba. He can't find you and that's a problem."

"I thought that's what we wanted."

"It was. I'm here now. How many has he killed?"

Keith answered. "Six."

"Six." Mag nodded. "And they're still looking for him? He hasn't jumped, because I have been following this and they haven't found his body yet. We need to get him before he jumps to another body or jumps into you again."

"Again?" I held up my hand. "You think this is the same entity?"

"I do."

"And you said jump? Mag, can he do that. I didn't know they could come through more than once."

Mag chuckled. "My dear, of course they can. And each time they do it, they get stronger. The only way to guarantee that they

166

never return is they need brought or thrown into what you would call damnation or hell," she said. "Basically, a soul incinerating place."

"How … how do we do that?"

"Only the soul of a light person can open the doorway to the incineration."

"Oh my God," I gasped. "One of us has to die?"

Keith pointed at Mag. "I vote her. She's older."

Mag huffed in irritation. "Neither of us. Being a light person isn't exclusive to our century or millennium." She turned and faced Galen. "Is it Spartan?"

My jaw dropped a little in the revelation of what she was saying. "Galen is or was a light person?"

"He's more than that," said Mag. "Since his passing, he has become a soldier of light. It's not your first time back, is it?"

Galen sheepishly lifted a finger. "It is however my first time being back and watching Golden Girls."

"He didn't happen upon you. Whatever reason he gave you," Mag stated. "He gets the call."

"Not by telephone," Galen clarified. "It's a message my head gets that a person is in danger or a bad entity has escaped. I am able to find a light person to bring me through and I end the problem. This is the first time that I was told a light person was pursued and arrived before the entity."

"This is amazing," I said. "Mag, did you know?"

"Not until I saw him," Mag replied. "I just remember the stories of a certain US senator was targeted by Hitler and a Spartan soldier ended that."

"It was not that easy," Galen replied. "The Hitler entity had been jumping for a long time, each time he was cast from the body, he went into the light. The last time was final. He is gone."

"Whoa," Keith commented. "You took him to the bowels of hell?"

"No." Galen shook his head. "I was able to cast him into the flames. Taking him in there would have been the end of my soul as well."

"And we don't want that," Mag said. "We need him to cast him into incineration. Once he is thrown from the earthly form, the light will come very fast. Three things could happen. He backs into the light to try again, jumps into a body or we open the gate. The final option is our only option."

"Then what's the plan?" I asked.

"I'm here now. I am confident. But you are safe and secret in here," Mag said. "And we can't have that. The only way to beat him is to draw him out. With me and Galen in the room, the guards outside—"

"And me," said Keith.

Mag only shifted her eyes at him and then continued. "With the safety measures in place, we have one choice. We call him out."

"How?" I asked.

"He's looking for you, trust me, he's looking. We just need to find a way to let him know where you are."

Following Mag's suggestion was dangerous, but I understood it had to be done and I had an idea on how to reveal my location.

THIRTY-TWO

JEREMY SPOKE IN CLASS

Donner Greg looked really handsome on television. The lighting was just right, the camera angle, too, and unlike when he was up close in person, the creases in the pancake makeup weren't seen. In fact, it was hard to tell he was wearing any.

I knew he was.

"And there you have it," Donner spoke as he walked the main street of Aurora. "It doesn't get any more Dateline than this. Jon P. Roth." A picture of the sleep technician appeared on screen. "Dashing, young, deviate ... murderer. He's on the lose while Harper Monroe, broken and bruised, sits in protective custody at Aurora General awaiting surgery tomorrow morning. I'm Donner Greg. Goodnight."

I aimed the remote and shut off the television.

"I counted four times," Galen said. "Four times that he gave your location."

"He did what we asked."

"What does the authority officer say?"

"Lenzi? Oh, he thinks we're crazy for doing this."

"I am here to protect from the spiritual realm, you have an officer just outside the door. I believe you are safe for now."

"When will he come?" I asked.

Galen shook his head. "I do not know that he will. If he is cunning, he will know it is a set up. We should prepare for the unexpected."

"I think you're right."

"Now, you try to rest. They slice into your flesh tomorrow. I am here."

"Sleep will be good. It'll take my mind off of being hungry."

"Goodnight, Harper."

"Goodnight, Galen."

I watched the good soldier move to the back of the room by the bathroom and I closed my eyes, turning to my left side.

I was tired and I didn't know if I would dream. I really wasn't worried about it. I was safe.

Worry and fear didn't cross my mind as I drifted off. That was until I crossed into a lucid dream and saw him.

It wasn't normal, it wasn't bright and sunny, nor was it in a plain room.

It was gloomy and dark, a feeling of overwhelming sadness just enveloped everything. Even he looked different – Jeremy.

Unlike other souls I had encountered, Jeremy didn't look at peace. He was pale. His green Henderson Brothers Tee shirt was saturated with blood and a huge gaping hole was in his neck.

"I'm sorry, Harper, I'm sorry," he said. "I didn't know it was him when he came to the bar. I didn't. Until he said things."

"I know. How could you?" I asked.

"I didn't. I swear." He shook his head. "I realized what was happening, you know? I grabbed my knife; thought I'd end it and he got me."

"Did he say why?"

"I knew too much. You knew too much. You always knew too much, you just didn't know it."

I shook my head. "That doesn't make sense."

"It never made sense," Jeremy said. "It was over, you know. But I guess it really never was."

Jeremy seemed to be talking in circles. I wasn't concerned until five figures appeared behind him. I couldn't make out who they were. They were shadowy and threatening like.

I felt it in my soul.

Wake up, I told myself.

"I know it doesn't seem it …" Jeremy walked to me. "But it has to be this way."

The arms of the figures reached around Jeremy for me.

I backed up, "Wake up."

"It won't seem it when you wake up. This is the only way it will work."

"What are you talking about?" I asked. "Wake up."

"He won't come to you while he's there. He needs him gone. He wants him gone." He touched my chest. "Wake up."

"Shit." I knew it. I didn't want him touching me, but when he said to wake up, I did.

Sure enough, as I feared, when I sat up, Jeremy was in the corner of the room not far from Galen. Standing there in all his bloody glory.

"I'm sorry, Galen," I told him.

"Me, too," Jeremy said, then looked at me. The light began to build behind him. "I'm not bad. I'm just not at rest. I have to do this. He needs to be strong."

Jeremy's words from the other side ran through my mind.

And it hit me.

He won't come to you while he's there. He needs him gone.

Jeremy was talking obviously about his brother. And the 'he' that Wes needed gone, had to be Galen.

"Galen," I said. "Move from him."

"The light is here." Galen drew his sword, stepping to Jeremy. "Spirit, go into the light."

"Galen," I warned. "Please step away from him. The light …"

"I can move from it." Galen glanced my way and pushed Jeremy with the tip of the sword. "Go into the light."

The light grew, beams of colors encompassed Jeremy like beautiful and colorful specks of orbs, dancing about.

"Gladly," Jeremy said stepping back. But as he did, the five figures appeared.

Their arms reached out at the same time as Jeremy.

The light grew enormous, taking over the whole wall near the bathroom.

"Galen!" I shouted.

Galen sliced forward with sword. It was like a laser beam of light going through the arms.

Only there were too many arms, and one of the hands locked on to Galen's sword.

Galen backed off, but the light was too strong.

He had nowhere to go.

The light had nearly reached the end of my bed.

Jeremy began to fade, one with the brightness. "It's the only way," he said.

On those final words, Galen looked at me. The light took over him like a wave, absorbing his being and then vanishing just as fast.

Empty.

Silent.

I felt my insides twist and turn, my heart raced out of control.

Suddenly terror swept over me. I knew what I had to face. What was ahead. How was I going to do it? How was I supposed to face and fight some other worldly being?

Especially now. Galen was gone.

THIRTY-THREE

SLICE OF LIFE

Mag wore a purple, shiny suit with a white blouse and a white corsage. Her hair was done up, she looked amazing. Like someone who was going to a really expensive Mother's Day brunch.

She paced back and forth in my room by the bathroom the next day. Looking at the wall, looking at me, then back again.

Keith stood by my bed. "I can't believe you lost him."

"I didn't lose him. The light took him."

"After he's been the master of running from it?"

"Where was he gonna go? Behind me?" I asked. "I highly doubt Galen would hide behind me."

"He wouldn't," Mag said. "It doesn't make sense. It truly doesn't. I mean … granted he wouldn't go behind you, but if Jeremy was making no moves to run from the light, then why did Galen get so close. This isn't his first time at the rodeo."

Keith shrugged "Maybe he was scared and didn't want to tell us. He saw the light and was like, 'yeah, you know what? Hard pass on fighting the evil entity'."

Both Mag and I gasped and looked at him.

"Just tossing out theories." Keith lifted his hands.

"Anyway." Mag walked to me and grabbed my hand. "No worries. You'll be fine in surgery. He's only getting through there in physical form, and the police can stop him. In fact, Officer

Lenzi is doing a sweep of the floor now. In the meantime, I will trance out and go to the other side and find someone. Maybe Elvis. He's a light soldier now." She tapped my hand and walked to the door, pausing. "Although the last time I brought him through it started this whole Elvis never died thing. See you when you get back. Good luck."

She walked out.

Keith glanced down to me. "It'll be fine. I promise. I don't think he's coming for you here."

"I don't know."

"Look, just do this and don't worry. When you wake from surgery, I'll have a supreme from Sam's Subs waiting for you."

"Thank you."

"And again, don't worry, it'll be fine. You have all these people watching out for you."

I nodded but kept thinking, 'everyone but Galen'.

I put on a good front, but the truth was, I was worried. I was going under the knife and under anesthesia. Sure, I was going to be in a safe room, but I was going to be in my most vulnerable state yet.

The hospital aide that rolled me down to the operating room, sang his own blues slash rap version of an Imagine Dragons' song. It was pretty cool, and I focused on that, listening to his originality

From my room to the elevator, all the way down he sang.

Prior to going down, a nurse came in and flushed my intravenous line for surgery.

I was more nervous about going into the operating room than I was about getting cut open and having a pin put in me.

It was a strange feeling trying to avoid watching the overhead lights as I moved down the halls.

The elevators were located by a window and the only time the hospital aide stopped singing is when he paused by the window.

"Man, lots of activity out there," he said.

"Activity?" I asked. "What do you mean?"

"Police."

I started to get scared.

"Think you can find out what happened?" I asked.

"I'll try, but you'll be in La-La land in little bit, you won't have to worry about it at all."

"Great." I grumbled and he brought me through the final corridor. I knew we were there by the police officer that stood outside the door. "Stop," I told the aide and looked at the police officer. "Where's Lenzi?"

"He'll be back," the officer replied. "He was checking on something outside."

"Okay. Okay, thanks," I said nervously.

The aide brought me in the surgery theater, rolling me over to the table, where a female nurse in hospital scrubs, helped transfer me to the operating table. She wore a mask and a cover on her head. I could tell by her eyes she was smiling.

"Thanks, Dan," she said to the aide.

Dan wished me good luck and rolled the gurney out of the room, closing the door.

It felt so cold and hollow in that room, the big light above my head.

The nurse adjusted the IV, then began hooking me up to the monitors.

"Calm down," she said. "It's gonna be fine."

"I'm just nervous."

"Of course. Just try to relax," she said, then looked to the door when a doctor walked in.

"Morning," he said.

"Morning, Doctor." She rolled a covered tray near my head. "Doctor Brewster is in the back scrubbing up."

"Good." He moved to my side. "I'm your anesthesiologist. Any history of reaction to anesthesia?"

"Not that I know of," I replied.

"Good." He uncovered the tray. "You'll get a sedative first and we'll monitor the anesthesia after you're out." He lifted the syringe. "We'll feed this into the line as soon as your surgeon comes in. Oh, sorry, I'm Doctor Marlin."

"Like the bar and grille?" I asked.

"Exactly. My father owns that."

"George is your father?"

He shook his head. "No, my uncle. My father wouldn't work there. It's crazy. We had a murder there last night."

"Yeah, I know, I was there."

"Wow. No wonder we have the police watching this room," he said.

"They think he is after me."

"Bet you're happy now." the nurse said.

"About him wanting to kill me?" I asked confused.

177

"No, about him being dead," she stated.

Doctor Marlin uncapped the syringe. "They got him?"

"No." She shook her head. "He shot himself right outside of the hospital."

"Shit," I whispered.

"It's okay." The nurse tapped my arm. "No worries."

Doctor Marlin turned his head to a clicking sound. "Hey Doctor Brewster. No need to lock that, they got the guy. Well, he got himself."

I shifted my eyes to see Doctor Brewster walk over to me. The nurse was just behind my head, Doctor Marlin to my right and Brewster approached the other side.

"We're about to administer the sedative," said Marlin.

Brewster just stood there. He peered down to me. "Hello, Harper."

That was when I knew.

The accent was gone.

Wes had jumped. He took Jon's life and jumped.

I saw the needle getting closer to my IV line and I freaked out.

"No! No!" I kicked my leg at Brewster and tried to get off the table.

"Harper," Marlin said. "Calm down."

Brewster laughed.

"Doctor!" the nurse scolded. "This isn't funny. We'll sedate her."

"No need," Brewster said eerily calm and lifted a scalpel from the tray.

"What the hell?" Marlin snapped. "What are you doing?" He dropped the syringe and it landed on my chest as he dove and reached for Brewster.

Brewster didn't hesitate or flinch, with a backwards swipe of his hand, he slit Marlin's throat.

The nurse screamed.

I had clarity. For a moment I knew what I had to do.

The blood poured from Marlin's wound and on to my stomach. I swiped up the syringe and swung out, plunging it into Brewster's stomach.

He grabbed my hair, lifting my head, the syringe still protruding from him.

The nurse tried to stop him, but he flung her away.

"Get help!" I yelled. "Get help!"

She ran, I know she did. I heard her crying and screaming, fighting to open the door and another scream as she left. Her scream fading.

Marlin stood there, half on the operating table, holding his throat, struggling to stop the bleeding. Just as Brewster was about to bring that scalpel to me, Marlin toppled on the table. His weight moved it enough that the blade went into his back.

I screamed, trying to get Marlin from me so I could flee.

Brewster lifted Marlin's limp body, tossing it aside then he lifted me. One hand tight to my throat. I tried to use my legs to lever myself.

I was choking, I thought my head would pull from my body.

Then I felt his fingers loosen. Brewster swayed.

The sedative had to be kicking in.

He teetered to the right, stumbled some and let go of me.

I didn't know if he toppled from the effects of the drug because when he dropped me, I bounced off the table and hit my head.

I was out.

THIRTY-FOUR

UNVEILING

Was I dead?

I thought for a moment that I was, that it was over.

I was in the operating room, able to see everything. I wasn't hovering, I was standing.

It was a mess. Doctor Marlin's body lay on the floor, blood splattered and smeared everywhere. I saw myself, laying there, my body wearing only a hospital gown, half twisted and turned.

Brewster struggled to fight the drug.

He sat on the floor, his back against the wall. His legs kicked as if he were fighting. But he wasn't out, he was doing everything he could not to fall under the sedative.

With a compelling force moving me more than I moved myself, I went through the door.

The police officer was slumped in the chair, a knife impaled his chest. The hallway was long and empty and the fluorescent overhead lights flickered and buzzed.

I wasn't in my realm, I was elsewhere.

Turning to my left I saw a set of double doors. I remembered going through them on the way to the OR.

I walked to those doors and pushed them. When I passed through, I wasn't in the hospital, I was in a little girl's room.

Two girls played Barbies.

One was Mya the other was Amanda.

Mya giggled. "What's your dolls name?"

"Amanda," Amanda answered.

Mya giggled again. "That's silly."

"Mya, come here," a man's voice called.

Mya quickly turned her head toward her bedroom door then back to Amanda. "Shh. Stay here. My mom's boyfriend doesn't know you're here. He doesn't like when I have friends over."

"Okay," Amanda answered.

Mya got up and left the room and Amanda continued to play.

The sound of the ticking wind up clock was loud. It was a Mickey Mouse clock on the white dresser, and it read that it was only one o'clock.

Then the arms of the clock moved fast and to the half past mark and Mya screamed. She didn't just scream, she cried out, "No, No," sobbing, begging for it to stop and then silence.

Amanda's eyes widened and she scooted back out of sight, hiding in the space between the bed and the dresser.

There was silence for just a short period of time, then the sound of footsteps rang out.

I could hear the sound of dragging and caught a glimpse of Wes as he moved by Mya's bedroom, pulling a bag.

Amanda kept her hands tightly over her own mouth, crying, scared, even when the door shut.

He left.

Why didn't she run? Why did she just hide there?

The clocked moved fast again, nearly an hour spun by.

"Mya, I'm home," the woman's voice called in the distance.

Amanda rushed from her hiding spot and out of the room. I followed her. The small hall led to the living room where the young mother set down her grocery bags when Amanda hugged her.

"What's wrong?" Mya's mother asked. "Where's Mya? I thought you two were playing?"

"She … she …."

The front door opened, and Wes walked in. He literally paused when he saw Amanda.

"What's going on?" Wes asked.

"Where's Mya?" the mother questioned.

Wes looked nervous. "She went to play with a friend."

"She was playing with Amanda in her room."

"She … she was here?" Wes pointed. "I didn't know."

"Well, I know how you are about that," Mya's mother said. "Do you know where Mya is."

"Strange thing." Wes stared coldly at the little girl. "Mya just left. Rude." He walked to Amanda and held out his hand. "I'll drive you home."

Amanda shook her head.

"It's okay," Mya's mother said. "Go on. I'll call your mom."

Wes grabbed hold of Amanda's hand and they walked out the door.

I ran. I ran as fast as I could to follow but when I stepped from the home, I was back there again.

Back again at the wooded area behind the church, watching once again as he strangled the life from little Amanda.

Just like before I heard the footsteps.

Only the voices were saying something different.

"I know he's up here. I saw," one man said.

"Are you sure?" asked a woman.

"Positive. I saw him with the body, when I went to go to the police, I saw him again with her. We have to hurry."

"It can't be," said the woman. "Mya's mother called …"

Wes slowly removed his hands from Amanda's neck.

"Harper, I'm sorry." The voice was close. "I'm sorry you had to see this again. It's the only way."

I turned my head and Jeremy stood there. He looked different. He wasn't bloody.

I backed up. "Why? Why are you doing this?"

"It had to be done. Can't you see?" Jeremy asked.

"I see that you are probably at peace now."

"Yeah." He nodded. "It's gonna be over. That's why I did it. He needed to be stronger."

I laughed almost through tears. "Stronger. Your brother is strong enough. You know that. Look what he's capable of."

"What are you talking about, Harper?"

"Your brother." I pointed to Wes.

"That's not my brother, Harper. Look again. Look again," Jeremy spoke strong. "Lift the veil and look."

In a blur everything seemingly rewound thirty seconds. It moved in reverse and played again.

Wes had his hands to the throat of Amanda. Her head turned toward me.

"Look close," said Jeremy. "Remember."

I looked again. Suddenly the face of Amanda changed. I saw her eyes staring at me. But it no longer was Amanda … it was me.

Eight-year-old me.

Everything wound back again, I was in Mya's living room. Watching it again. I was the little girl standing close to Mya's mother.

"I'll drive you home." He held out his hand to me.

"Go on," Mya's mother said.

In a flash I was back in those woods, he slowly pulled his hand from my neck. And then I saw him. It wasn't Wes.

It was my Uncle Earl.

"Go on, go with your uncle. I'll call your mom."

I gasped, my hand shooting to my mouth when I saw. I shook my head. It wasn't real.

"It's a trick."

"It's not a trick," Jeremy said. "It's what you buried and chose not to remember."

My Uncle Earl pulled back from my lifeless body. But I wasn't dead. I coughed and choked just as he reached for his pant buckle.

He paused and turned his head.

"No! No!" a woman screamed. "You son of a bitch! I'll kill you."

She charged to him holding a baseball bat and as she swung down nailing him that first time in the side of the head, I saw that woman was my mother.

Three men raced behind her. No one stopped her. They just grabbed me and pulled me away.

My mother was enraged, the look on her face was frightening. She battered down on her own brother, blasts to the head. One after another, cries of pain from her soul bellowing out with each strike to his skull.

It was like hitting a wet sponge, every strike just splattered more blood.

They let her go until she stopped on her own, dropped the bat, fell to her knees and sobbed.

Nothing was recognizable to his head. A mush pile. His arm did this twitching thing but there was no way he was alive.

One of the three men walked over to my mother.

The one that held on to me was a young Wes. Another younger man stood by him, clearly that was Jeremy.

My mother cried. "What do I do? What do I do now?"

"Don't worry," Wes said. "We'll take care of it. Don't worry."

"We got you, Mare," Jeremy added. "Take your baby home. She seems okay."

I turned from the scene of the past to the older version of Jeremy before me.

"Earl is strong," Jeremy said. "He goes back and forth and hurts people. He found you again and he was stopping at nothing until he got you and your mother. He got me. Now you need to get him gone for good. Wake up and do it."

"You took Galen."

"To make him stronger. Each time he comes back he gets stronger. It was the only way. Now wake up, Harper."

"Harper," I heard Galen's voice. "Wake up."

I did.

THIRTY-FIVE

EASY DOES IT

Pounding.

That was the first thing I heard.

Loud pounding, banging, it was steady.

"Open up! We'll get in!" voices shouted from outside.

I opened my eyes. I was alive, still on that floor. Marlin's body was inches from my feet and Brewster pushed another item against the operating room door.

Bang. Bang. Bang.

Help was outside the door, trying to get to us. They hit the door with something to break it in. But would they in time.

Slowly I managed to sit up. My head throbbed and I brought my hand to the back of my skull. It was wet, I was bleeding.

Trying to assess the situation, I looked around. What could I use as a weapon?

His attention was on the door. Quickly I pushed from my mind that it was the surgeon, Doctor Brewster. He looked like him, but I knew it was Earl.

Pain seared from my hip down my leg and around my back as I tried to move. Using my hands, I pulled myself up some, but slipped on Marlin's blood and something toppled to the floor causing a crashing sound.

Bang. Bang. Bang.

Uncle Earl turned, faced me and smiled. "Well, you're up."

"You shouldn't be."

"Dosage was for you. Not strong enough for me. But now you're awake. I was waiting. It won't be fun to kill you if you don't see it coming."

I grabbed hold of the operating table and used it as leverage to stand.

He laughed. "So pathetic."

"I know who you are."

"It's about damn time. You thought I was Wes, didn't you?"

I didn't say anything.

"Bastard. He tried to get me on the other side. Tossed his ass into the soul eater." He moved to me. "That's what we call it."

Bang. Bang. Bang.

A slight crack rang out and he hurriedly looked at the door.

"I don't have time. I'm back, thank you," he said.

"You were my uncle," I said, holding on to the table. "Why would you do this?"

"Why?" He laughed. "Harper, you're the reason I got caught. You're the reason I'm dead."

"No, you are. The Henderson brothers saw you with Mya's body. It was just a matter of time."

"You knew I killed Mya. Started the whole thing. I didn't mean to jump into your body when you were fourteen. I meant to go into your mom, have her kill you, whole slew of justice for me. But, shit happens." He shrugged. "I had fun in you. Did you know we strangled a three-year-old boy at the Shopmart? They sent you away for that to a mental institution."

I shook my head. Inching back from him.

Bang. Bang. Bang. Crack.

He looked at the door. "Okay, well, time to end this tit for tat."

"And then what? You can't stay in here forever."

"Yep, Doctor Brewster will go down, but his soul, my soul will live on."

I tried. I tried so hard to get away, but I was physically unable to move fast enough. My legs wouldn't work, it was so painful. I gave it my best, but Earl lunged for me and grabbed me.

He placed both of his hands on my face squeezing my cheeks. "Goodbye, Harper."

Bang. Bang. Bang. Boom.

The door blasted open, it was loud, and it startled him.

Lenzi rushed in extending his gun.

Earl's grip to my face had released enough that I gave everything I had, all of my might, and shoved him back.

"Shoot him!" I screamed.

Lenzi listened and didn't hesitate. He fired. Sequential shots, one, two, three, four, five.

Arms outward with a smile on his face, Earl jolted with each hit he took. On the final shot he dropped to the floor.

Within a second, my Uncle Earl's being emerged. Full form, hideous in nature. A reflection of the true soul that he was.

Earl looked at me, smiled then looked at Lenzi. A light formed behind him, ready to claim him and I watched in horror as Earl pounced his being, like a cat to his prey, toward Lenzi.

Inches away from consuming and possessing my new friend, I felt and heard the 'woosh' of air and warmth come from behind me.

Galen.

He shot passed me. At lightning speed, he speared shoulder first into Earl sailing him across the room.

Both ghostly beings slammed into the wall bouncing back. The light grew brighter, and Galen locked his arm around Earl's neck, reached for his sword and threw it toward the light.

The spear spun end over tip and the moment it hit the light, the light transformed.

No longer was it bright and beautiful.

The beams of color that once shot out were now replaced with flames.

Flames of red and blue encircled a dim white light, and it took up the entire wall.

Earl struggled, but he was no match for the strength and speed of Galen.

Galen locked a hold on a struggling Earl. One arm around his neck, the other around his torso and he backed up toward the fiery opening.

"No." I shook my head. "No. Don't go in there, Galen. Don't. Toss him."

Galen stood there holding Earl. He gave a closed mouth smile. "It's the only way to ensure he will not escape again."

"Galen …" I reached out my hand.

A loud chorus of damnation screams rang out, howling, screeching. The flames whipped out like arms, grabbing on to Galen as he stepped backwards.

Galen bowed his head slightly. "Goodbye, Harper. It has been an honor."

It rapidly swallowed Galen and Earl, then it all just stopped.

Complete and utter silence.

Lenzi breathed heavily and hurried to me. "Are you okay? I'm sorry. I should have been here sooner."

"It's alright. It's over. It's really over," I said.

My Uncle Earl's soul would never return. It was destroyed, consumed, and gone forever.

Unfortunately, so was Galen's.

THIRTY-SIX

TRICKS OF THE TRADE

There was something about seeing my mother that immediately caused the old country song, "Goodbye Earl' to play in my head.

The debacle in the operating room delayed me from going back to my room for hours. I had questions to answer, statements to give, all while I was dealing with physical and emotional pain.

Not wanting to give into the paranormal aspects of everything, they'd leave that to Donner Greg, the chief said the medical examiner was suspecting it was some sort of parasite that made both Jon and Doctor Brewster go insane.

Despite being given a replay of a traumatic moment in my life, I still didn't remember it. I didn't recall playing with Mya at all or when my Uncle Earl tried to kill me.

Did I ever remember it when I was younger? Was it something I blocked in my later years or when it happened?

My mother would answer that. At least I hoped she would.

Of course, I didn't get the surgery, it was rescheduled to happen in two days. The doctor that examined me said if I didn't need the pin, I needed it now.

I'd stay in the hospital until surgery day. Mag insisted I deserved that queen's room and paid for my stay.

Then again, there were no more armed guards. I wasn't in danger any longer. I felt that.

Describing my emotional state was hard. A part of me was relieved, another part sad and confused.

"I wish you would have told me you broke your hip." My mother stood at my bedside, talking to me and brushing my hair from my face like she did when I was a little girl.

She felt sorry for me, I could see it in her face. I knew that Mag had filled her in. How much or how little remained to be seen, but I'd find it out later.

"Does Dad know?"

"Know what?" she asked with a smile.

No one else was in the room at that moment, it was just me and her. So, I asked. "That you killed Uncle Earl."

My mother sighed heavily, pulled up a chair and sat down. "No. He doesn't and he never well. He believed the story like everyone else."

"No one ever suspected you?"

She shook her head. "After a while, you know, I started to think maybe I didn't do it.'"

"Oh, you did. I saw. You Neganed him."

"I'm sorry, I what?"

"Never mind," I told her. "What was the story? I didn't really get that."

"After I, you know, Uncle Earl, the Hendersons took his body down by the river and left him. They went to the police to let them know they saw Earl with Mya. A shoestring on her neck and he ran when they saw him."

"And the police bought that?"

My mother nodded. "They had seen him with another missing girl, and they suspected him of her disappearance. Mya never disappeared; she was murdered."

"Did you tell them what happened to me?"

"I told the chief on the side. He didn't need my testimony. The Hendersons weren't the only one that saw him carry that bag to the woods. They focused more on him being responsible and finding clues to the other girls. More so than who did the lynching. Without us, his family, pushing for justice, they didn't look too much into who did it. They assumed the Hendersons and their buddies lynched him."

"Aunt Connie? Does she know?"

"No. This is the first time I had spoken about it in ten years. Once and a while I'd call Jeremy to just talk."

"Did you know that Uncle Earl had possessed me?"

My mother tilted her head. "I didn't know, I suspected. Everyone thought I was nuts to think you weren't you. But when he strangled that boy in the supermarket with a shoestring, I knew … I knew. That's when the chief played a big role into getting you to Maine."

I slowly shook my head. "I can't remember any of it, I can't."

"I hope you never do."

"I know your religion keeps you from thinking this gift is good."

"Oh, it can do good," she said. "Mag helped you."

"So then you were hardcore for me to give it up because of Earl?"

My mother nodded. "Yes, Mag said he could come back if you ever opened that door again. So we did everything in our power to keep it shut."

"He's gone now. For good. He'll never come back."

"That's what Mag said."

I looked past my mother when I heard the knock on the door. Keith and Mag stood there.

"Come in," I said.

I could smell the food before Keith even held up the bag. Sam's Subs carried a distinct pleasant aroma that I called the best car freshener.

"As promised," Keith dangled the bag and walked to me. "How's it going Mrs. Monroe?"

"My daughter has a broken hip because of you, how do you think it's going?'

"Bad."

My mother grumbled then smiled at Mag. "Thank you again for all that you have done for my daughter."

"I'm here for her any time. No matter what she chooses to do."

My mother's smile strained. "What do you mean? Chooses to do."

"Yeah," Keith repeated. "What do you mean? You told her to stop."

"I did. I was adamant because I knew about Earl. But," Mag said, "Harper has a gift that goes way beyond what I can do. She doesn't need to go to the other side and yank someone back like Freddy Kruger. I never had spirits come to me for help. That's a whole other level."

My mother shook her head. "It's dangerous."

"There are ways to do it safely. Find another Galen, or don't cross over. She can control when she does that," Mag explained. "Prazosin for at night and wine or whiskey to stop the trances. I must warn you though, you'll get one hell of a tolerance."

"So, wait," Keith interjected. "Are you saying she can do the paranormal stuff safely?"

"She'll have to learn to do it safely. I can teach her."

"Yes, sweet." Keith clenched his fist. "Our videos will keep going viral."

"No." My mother shook her head. "No. I know I can't make you do anything, but Harper, tell me you're done with this."

"I don't know," I replied. "Mom, I helped families find peace. I can do good with this. I need to do something. I feel like … I don't know, my whole life I didn't have direction and a lot of that had to do with this gift that was buried."

"Dude, we will make a shit load of money," Keith said.

"I really don't care about money. I don't." I shook my head. "It's about finding a purpose. And honestly, if I can find a way to do this right, to use this gift without getting hurt …" I said, "I have to try."

I didn't realize how strongly I felt about it at that moment until I realize I had a choice.

Give it up or learn to use it safely.

And like I told Keith, I had to try.

THIRTY-SEVEN

SUSPICIOUS MINDS

SEVEN MONTHS LATER

Lenzi grunted as he set down the box on the reception table near the front door. He acted as if it weighed a ton.

"Where do you want this?" Lenzi asked.

"Um. I don't know." I replied. "Just put it in my office."

My office.

I couldn't believe we were finally moving into the new building. Of course, I had Mag to thank. She funded everything, claiming she had more money than she knew what to do with.

Whenever she did government work, it paid a fortune.

I was more than a government worker, although I helped her out, I really wanted to see if I could help people. It turned out I could.

When I was in the hospital so many well wishes came in along with requests for help.

I had to find a way to help people without always trancing out or going to the other side.

Again, I had Mag to thank. She was a great teacher.

Luciano's had some revelation about me and asked me to come back to my job. They sent so much food to the hospital, I became the staff's favorite patient.

I politely turned them down. I didn't tell them it was because they fired me, I used my hip as an excuse.

When I got out of the hospital Mag put me in training to hone in on my gifts.

I stayed at my mother's house while I healed and learned.

Lenzi was foremost in asking for help and bringing me cases.

Missing persons, children, and adults.

Sadly, I found four in the first month, drawing them from the other side. It seemed my light was a calling card, and they came to me.

At first it was freaky, but I learned to handle it.

There was a bright side. I did find a missing husband who wasn't dead. His deceased mother-in-law came to me to let me know where he was hiding.

There was truly very little money in the work I did, so I would take a job once a month with Mag.

That enabled me to open the center.

The Monroe Investigators and Study Center.

We went from my mother's basement office to a building across the street from Henderson Tires.

It was a big building, but we needed it.

My father had painted a lot of the rooms for me and was glad to help.

He helped Doctor Strauss get his area ready first. Doctor Strauss took up half the building but needed the space. He was so floored by what happened to me, he decided he was going to study lucid dreams and the connection to the other side.

I was surprised how many 'lucid dream' studies he had scheduled.

It was move in day, at least it was for me, so it was a bit hectic.

I looked at the box Lenzi set down. "Yeah, I'll put this in my office. You know as soon as I can, I am hiring you here."

"As soon as you can match my police officer salary, I'm in."

"We have a lot of cases to sort through."

"I'm always here to help," he said.

I lifted the boxes.

"Whoa," my mother called out. "Wait. What is in that box?"

Lenzi answered. "Photos of people she helped. It's not many, but Harper wanted to collect them."

"Yes, so we can make a wall." My mother pointed to the bare wall near the door. "Right here. So, people can see who my daughter helped."

"So, leave it here?" Lenzi asked.

"Yes, I'll handle it. And Harper. Doctor Strauss is looking for you. When you go, please tell Keith to turn that horrible music down."

"Yes, Ma'am," I replied and looked at Lenzi. "I'll talk to you in a bit."

"Drinks later?" Lenzi asked.

Before I could answer, my mother did. "Yes. It keeps her grounded and as long as she doesn't drive."

"There you have it," I said.

"Harper." My mother pointed. "Strauss. He's a busy man."

"On it." I told Lenzi I'd see him later and headed to see Strauss before my office.

My mother.

She went from reluctant and fearful to in control. Then again, I had to make a deal with her.

If I did continue to use my gift, I had to make her my office manager and find a light soldier for protection.

Both terms I agreed to.

Mag helped me find a light soldier. He was always ready and waiting. He told me he was going to hang out a lot in my new office if Strauss didn't have anyone interesting. He was nice enough, not as tough as Galen. He was there and I was safe. That was his job.

Doctor Strauss had his new sleep study lab on the second floor, and I could hear the really bad country music that played from the lab.

As soon as I poked in my head, Keith turned down the music.

"Did you want to see me?" I asked Doctor Strauss.

"Yes, Harper, I have a very interesting study tonight. I really think she may be hitting the other side. Can you be here?"

"Sure." I folded my arms and nodded. "No problem."

"And your light soldier."

"He'll be here. What else does he have to do? I'll be by tonight."

"Oh, Harp, wait," Keith called my name as I turned. "I have something for you."

I backed up.

Keith raced to his desk, lifted a frame, and brought it to me. "My friend finished. I hope this helps and I hope you like it."

It was wrapped like a present and as I unraveled the picture in the frame, I knew it was no less than a gift.

Keith's friend the artist. The same one that took the ghostly image of Cherrie and made her image into a photo of a little girl, took the ghostly image of Galen and made it into a masterpiece.

I was in awe and breathless.

"You like it?" Keith asked.

"I love it."

"I know you use photos to find people."

Doctor Strauss stepped into the conversation. "You're still trying?"

I nodded, staring at the picture. "I am. I'll keep trying."

"Even though Mag said—"

I cut off Doctor Strauss. "Mag is wrong this time. I believe it. She's wrong."

Doctor Strauss touched my arm. "Then you'll do it. What about your Light Soldier?"

"He'll deal," I said. "I'll see you tonight." After glancing once more at the picture, I looked and smiled at Keith. Then I left them both to go to my new office.

It was an exceptional image, it reminded me a bit of that Spartan movie poster, but it was Galen.

Mag insisted his soul was gone, destroyed in a self-sacrifice to rid the universe of Earl.

I believed that fate had a backup plan on those sorts of things.

Good spirits, beings, soldiers, didn't just go away forever. That couldn't be the case.

Plus, I felt it. I felt it deep in my gut that Galen wasn't gone for good. That his spirit wasn't destroyed along with Earl.

I knew Earl was gone, it made sense and felt right.

But not with Galen.

If I was going to continue helping people, reaching out to the other side and having the other side reach me, I needed a light soldier.

Of course, I had one. There was nothing wrong with him. He just wasn't Galen.

I needed and wanted Galen to be there to be the one watching over me.

It didn't matter how long it took; I was confident that I would find him. We would be an unstoppable force that helped a lot of people.

I was sure of it.

In the meantime, Elvis would have to do.

About the Author

Author Jacqueline Druga brings to you the world's end in every way imaginable through the pages of her novels.

While best known for her apocalyptic works, Jacqueline's works expand many genres, including Humor, YA, Romance, Sci-fi and Thriller.

Jacqueline prides herself on being down to earth and light-hearted.

A mother and grandmother, Jacqueline absorbs and loves every single moment that she is writing and invites you to share in her world.

Visit her website: www.jacquelinedruga.com